HELLER FROM TEXAS

HELLER FROM TEXAS

William Heuman

GUNSMOKE

First published in the US by Fawcett Gold Medal

This hardback edition 2013
by AudioGO Ltd
by arrangement with
Golden West Literary Agency

ISBN 978 1 471 32130 6

British Library Cataloguing in Publication Data available.

Printed and bound in Great Britain by
MPG Books Group Limited

Chapter One

IT WAS a little after dusk when Trev Buchman raised
the lights of Rawdon just as he was coming over Wind
Hill. As he remembered it, he was now about abreast
of old Joe Fineran's shack along Squaw Creek, and if he'd
wanted to he could have stopped off there for a bite to eat,
that is, if the nester were still living. It had been eight
years, Trev remembered, and in eight years a lot could
happen. Old men like Fineran sickened and died; men
like Trev's brother Jim did it the hard way, by falling off
a holding corral fence after a dizzy spell, and being
trampled to death by the milling crowd of cattle inside.

Trev Buchman thought about that, and even thinking
about it was revolting. It had been a hell of a way to
die, but that was the way it had been according to the
stories he'd heard down in Flint Rock seventy-five miles
to the south.

Box B, once the biggest spread east of Cannon River,
and ruled with an iron and ruthless fist by big Bull Buchman, had now passed into the hands of Jim's widow,
whom Trev had never seen. It had been eight years since
he'd had it out with his father and ridden off never
to return.

They'd told him down in Flint Rock that Jim had been
married to this girl for a year and a half before his death,
and that she was a looker, which had rather surprised
him because Jim had been the plodding type, taking it

5

from his domineering father, keeping his temper, unlike Trev who'd always fought back at him. Jim, who'd been three years older, had not been a ladies' man, either. He'd very seldom gone to the dances in town, dances which had usually ended in fist fights and brawls started by Trev Buchman and other young hellers from the Cannon Basin.

At twenty-eight, Trev remembered those days not with nostalgia, but with curiosity, and that was the reason he'd headed north four years after his father had passed away. It was idle curiosity which was bringing him back to the Cannon Basin, and Rawdon, and people he'd known. He'd wanted to see Jim, too, because they'd gotten along tolerably well as youngsters, and he'd thought Jim would be glad to see him, but he'd come six weeks too late.

Trev let the gray gelding take its time going down the grade on the other side of Wind Hill. He sat loosely in the saddle, a tall man, not as big as his father, nor as heavy in the shoulders—Bull Buchman had been a giant of a man—but he was big, and he was solid, thinning out in the shanks. The dust of the trail was on him, and he'd lost some weight because he'd come over eight hundred miles up from Texas where he'd been at various times a free rider, a bouncer in a saloon, a peace officer, and a free-lance range detective.

Moving down the grade, he again had the peculiar, intangible feeling that someone was riding behind him. He'd felt that way for almost an hour since the sun had gone down. He had heard no hoofbeats, and looking back several times, he'd seen nothing, but yet the uneasiness persisted. From working much alone as a peace officer and a range detective, he'd gradually developed a kind of sixth sense which told him when awareness was necessary.

He had no enemies in this part of the country, and there were no law officers on his trail now. If a rider was behind him, the matter could be simply coincidental. Trev Buchman decided to see if his senses were playing tricks on him.

At the bottom of the grade, on the right side of the road, was a stand of cottonwoods along the edge of the trickle that was Squaw Creek. He remembered that farther down along this same creek, past Joe Fineran's place and across a big meadow, there were some pools where as a boy, he'd fished with the old man. He wondered if

Joe Fineran still fished those pools for the big rainbow trout.

Trev turned the gray off the road and in among the trees. He sat there, motionless, facing the road, one hand resting idly on the horn of the saddle, and he watched the dim rim of the hill against the night sky.

He sat there for several minutes, and he was beginning to think that this time he'd been deceived, when he saw a rider swing up over the hill and start down the other side.

He forgot about the rider the next moment, however, when a scattering of shots came from the direction of Fineran's shack. The sounds exploded suddenly against the still of the night, and the gray horse, accustomed to gun firing, moved uneasily, nevertheless.

Trev's gun came out of the holster almost without his thinking about it, but he remained where he was, knowing that it was the height of foolishness for a man to ride into the middle of gunplay, especially at night when neither friend, nor foe, nor stranger, could be distinguished.

He could hear horses running in the night, then, and he counted two of them, coming in his direction. As far as he remembered, only Joe Fineran's place was up along Squaw Creek, and it was ridiculous to think that the old nester would be involved in a shooting scrape of any kind. Fineran had been a mild, seedy little man without enemies. Bull Buchman, usually a rough one on nesters, had permitted Fineran to scratch up an acre or two of bottom land along the creek, and grow his corn and the few vegetables upon which he subsisted. Trev did not think Fineran had ever even shot a gun in his life, and it was inconceivable to think that someone had been shooting at him.

The riders were coming down along the creek, heading in for the road, and they passed within fifteen feet of where Trev sat astride the gray. He could see them only as dark shapes in the night. He could ascertain in the starlight only the fact that one horse had white markings on it.

Squaw Creek swung sharply when it reached the road, and then moved parallel with it. Then two riders hammered out into the road, and kept going in the direction of Rawdon.

Trev hesitated for one moment, not sure whether he ought to follow the riders, or head back in the direction of Fineran's place. He decided upon the latter course. If old Joe had been hit he might need help, but still Trev found it impossible to conceive of anyone throwing lead at Joe Fineran. The man had nothing which another would want; he would never willingly offend anyone, and Bull Buchman, years ago, had given his riders orders to let Fineran be.

Moving the gray out of the trees, Trev pushed up along the creek in the direction of the shack. He gave one passing thought to the rider who had been behind him, and who, like himself, had undoubtedly frozen and drifted off the road at the sound of the shots.

Fineran's place lay less than three hundred yards from the road, and Trev could see the lamplight in the oil-cloth window as he came up closer. He remembered that Fineran had had a dog, an old white mongrel which had undoubtedly died in the interval that Trev had been here last. No dog came out to meet him as he rode up, and dismounted near a pole corral where Fineran had kept a flea-bitten horse in the old days.

"Joe!" Trev called. "Joe Fineran?"

The door of the shack was open, and the yellow lamp-light fell across the smooth, hard-packed dirt outside, but Joe Fineran didn't answer.

Trev started forward. He took about three steps before he stumbled across a limp form on the ground.

"Joe?" he said.

He could hear the man breathing heavily on the ground, and when he got his hands under the armpits and pulled the body into the light, he could see that Joe Fineran had gotten into his first shooting scrape, his first, and undoubtedly his last. His whole white shirtfront was stained with blood, and blood was coming from his mouth.

"Take it easy, Joe," Trev murmured, and he wished now that he'd gone after the two riders who'd set out toward Rawdon. A savage hatred began to build up inside him for the two killers. He was remembering the afternoons he'd fished those pools with this gentle man on the ground, listening to him talk of fish, and of life in general.

"When your time's comin', boy," Joe used to say, "it's comin'. Ain't no use tryin' to run from it."

The time was coming now to this small, seedy, shriveled man in his sixties, with a tuft of white hair and a thin neck, and blood trickling down the stubble on his chin.

Trev picked him up and carried him into the shack, putting him down on the cot along one wall. He tore open the bloody shirt, and he saw the three bullet holes, and then he started to curse softly, and he was cursing when Joe Fineran opened his eyes.

The nester looked straight at Trev for a moment, and then he said, puzzled, "Jim?"

Trev shook his head. "Trev," he said. "I'm back, Joe."

Joe Fineran moved a feeble hand on the cot. "Trev," he breathed. "Hells bells!"

"Who got you, Joe?" Trev asked him. "You see them?"

Fineran was going fast, and Trev wasn't sure he'd get the words out.

"Fogarty," he breathed finally. "Red Fogarty."

Fineran's pale blue eyes were on the ceiling, and they were moving back—back toward the wall behind him.

"Trev," Fineran murmured again. "Welcome home."

Then he was gone. His eyes stopped moving, and the labored breathing stopped, and he was gone. Trev sat beside him, and then he looked at the lamp on the table nearby, and then he took off his hat.

He wondered why it had had to be this way. This was a man who had moved along in the quiet waters close to the shore. He should have died in his bed this way, but not with bullet holes in him, and his boots still on.

A man by the name of Fogarty had killed him. He'd said that without any hesitation at all, indicating that he'd clearly seen his assailant. The name meant nothing to Trev, but then Rawdon, and the Cannon Basin would now be full of names which meant nothing to him. Red Fogarty meant something now, though. It meant a murderous killer who had shot down an old man who, even if he'd been armed, was no match for anyone.

Trev looked around the one room in which Fineran had lived for the past fifteen-or-so years. There was not much to it. He'd done his cooking on a battered iron cookstove he'd retrieved from some dump heap. He had a rough board table and a chair in the room, and this cot in one corner, and a shelf with a few groceries on it.

There were no guns. Trev picked up the lamp and

walked out into the night with it. He searched on the ground near where he'd stumbled over Joe Fineran's body, but he found nothing. The old man had been unarmed when he'd been shot down, probably having come out of his shack by a summons from the man who went by the name of Fogarty.

In the lamplight he could see the hoofprints made by the two horses. They'd been very close up to where Fineran was shot. He could see no bootprints, indicating that the two men had not even dismounted when they'd opened up on the defenseless man.

A horse was coming down the creek, moving at a leisurely pace, and Trev immediately blew out the lamp and slipped his gun from the holster. He backed up into the shadows along the wall of the shack and he waited, still holding the lamp in one hand.

He saw the rider come into sight, a vague form against the dark background of the hills beyond. The rider skirted the pole corral, and then stopped and waited.

Trev said, "All right. Come easy."

The rider was less than ten yards away now, sitting motionless on his horse, and Trev was positive this was the man who'd been behind him on the stage road.

"Heard the shots," the rider said succinctly. "Anybody hurt?"

"Man dead," Trev told him. He still held the gun in his hand, but he set the lamp down on the doorstep outside the shack.

The rider was dismounting, tying his horse to the corral, and he came forward slowly now, Trev's gun still on him.

"Have a match?" Trev asked. "Put it to this lamp on the ground."

"You don't have a match?" The stranger chuckled.

"Reckon we'll use yours," Trev told him.

A match flared up a moment later, and the stranger came up to lift the lamp globe and put the match to the wick. He replaced the globe, and Trev had a good look at his face.

He was a thin, wiry man with a lean face and a sharp hooked nose. His chin was narrow, too, and his hands were long, slender, supple. He was dressed in black and he wore a black, flat-crowned Stetson.

"Who's the dead man?" he asked, and Trev knew him immediately to be a stranger in this part of the country.

Everyone in the Cannon Basin knew the nester Joe Fineran and they knew where he was holed up.

"He went by the name of Fineran," Trev explained. "A nester."

"You knew him?"

Trev stared back at the man over the lamp. "I knew him," he said.

The thin man grinned, revealing yellowed teeth. "It wasn't you," he said. "Saw two riders come out onto the road."

"You behind me heading into Rawdon?" Trev asked him.

"Knew there was somebody up ahead," the thin-faced man nodded. He added thoughtfully, "Reckon I wasn't followin' you, mister."

Trev picked up the lamp and turned to go into the shack with it. He said over his shoulder, "The name's Buchman. Trev Buchman."

He remembered, then, that he didn't have to identify himself any more in this part of the country because there was only one Buchman left. The heller, they'd called him when he was younger. He'd been the prodigal who'd left home, and Jim had been the dutiful son who'd remained, only to fall off a corral fence and die. It added up to exactly nothing.

The thin man behind him said laconically, "McTigue."

That was all. The name had a vaguely familiar ring to it, and it was the kind of name Trev knew he could have heard in any saloon or any gambling hall in the West, and yet never connect with any particular person. It was a name which did not need a handle before it; it was just McTigue, and the thin man had said it as if he understood that Trev would recognize it.

"You're not from this part of the country," Trev said as McTigue walked over to look down at the dead man.

"No," McTigue said. He glanced around the room, and then he said, "This man have a gun?"

"No gun," Trev told him.

"Just shot him down?"

"You see him," Trev said grimly.

"Hell of a business," McTigue murmured, and he walked to the door to stand there, looking out into the night as he rolled a cigarette. "Know who did it?" he asked over his shoulder.

"I know," Trev said.

McTigue turned to look at him then as if this information surprised him. "You know?" he repeated.

"I know," Trev said again.

"What do you figure on doin'?"

"Shoot him on sight," Trev said. "I expect that to be tonight."

McTigue's thin, angular face cracked into a smile. "Reckon you're a rough one," he murmured. "Heard of Bull Buchman, and a Jim Buchman up this way. You're a new one. Related?"

"Jim was my brother," Trev told him.

McTigue had turned and was watching Trev through a cloud of tobacco smoke from his cigarette.

"Down in Flint Rock," he said, "they say your brother died kind of unnatural."

Trev was throwing a blanket over Joe Fineran's body. He didn't say anything to that.

"His widow got Box B," McTigue went on softly. "She wasn't a Buchman."

Trev turned to look at him. "I didn't come up here for that," he said quietly.

McTigue shrugged. "Who the hell knows why a man comes or goes anywhere." He smiled. "Just makin' talk. Mind if I ride in to Rawdon with you?"

Trev bent down over the lamp to blow out the flame. "Come ahead," he said. Then the room was in darkness, and he could only see the glow of McTigue's cigarette, and he heard McTigue say softly, "Reckon there'll be a little excitement up that way tonight, Buchman. I like excitement."

Chapter Two

THEY RODE into Rawdon at about nine o'clock that night, and coming into the main street, Trev could see that it had nearly doubled in size. There were many new stores, at least twice as many saloons, and a new hotel on the corner of the main street. It was to be expected, though. During the past eight years Rawdon had become a railroad town and it was now the central cattle shipping point for a radius of more than three hundred miles. Trev had a glimpse of the holding pens down along the railroad siding.

There were people in town this night, also, and Trev remembered suddenly that it was Saturday night. All the loose riders would be in from the surrounding ranches. A man by the name of Red Fogarty would be here because Fogarty had ridden away from Joe Fineran's shack thinking that no one had observed him, and believing Fineran to be dead when he'd left.

McTigue said casually, "Bigger than it was, Buchman?"

"It's grown." Trev nodded. "You been here before?"

"Passed through," McTigue murmured. "Where do you start?"

Trev looked across at him as they moved their mounts past the first few saloons.

"What do you mean?" he asked.

"Reckon you're lookin' for a man." McTigue smiled. "Figured I'd ride along to see the fun." He added, "There were two of them up at that shack. You might need a cover."

"How are you in this?" Trev asked him. "You didn't know Fineran."

"Maybe I didn't like the way he died," McTigue told him. "Maybe I just like to see a fight."

Trev frowned slightly. He still didn't know how to take this thin-faced man astride the rather jaded little blue roan. McTigue was a man of enigmas, and Trev was almost inclined to believe that this was the real reason for McTigue's trailing along.

13

They turned in at the Fairfax Stables, both men giving the hostler instructions to feed and rub down the mounts. They went out on the street, Trev still not having seen anyone he knew.

McTigue said, "Eat first?"

"Later," Trev told him.

That grin came to McTigue's face again. "My kind of man," he murmured as they moved down the street.

There was a saloon at the corner called The Big Western which Trev remembered from earlier days. The place had been renovated, however, and there were now four bartenders up at the bar instead of the usual two. Every card table was filled, and they had to take a place at the far end of the bar for their drinks.

McTigue said, "Know anybody?"

"Not yet," Trev told him, and then he heard a wild whoop behind him.

A little man with rust-colored hair, and a flattened nose had hopped up from one of the card tables and was coming toward them, grinning from ear to ear, hand outstretched.

"Trev!" the little man whooped. "Trev Buchman!"

McTigue said softly, "Reckon they know you're home now, Buchman."

Men at the card tables had turned around to look at him curiously. A sudden silence came to the bar. Men at the far end stepped back to look in Trev's direction.

The little man with the rust-colored hair was pumping Trev's hand.

"How's it, Charlie," Trev said.

Charlie Brackett had ridden for Box B in the old days, and he'd been one of Trev's stand-bys when they'd gotten into brawls at the dance hall. Charlie had always been loyal to Box B, and even more so to Trev Buchman.

"Eight years," Charlie grinned. "Eight helluva long years."

He signaled for the bartender to bring them drinks, but Trev called out to the bartender: "Make it three."

"Three?" Charlie Brackett murmured.

Trev stepped back from the bar. "McTigue," he said. "Meet Charlie Brackett."

Little Charlie looked at McTigue, the dislike plain in his homely face. Charlie had bright blue eyes to go with the smashed nose and the reddish hair, and he was not a man who could conceal his feelings.

"Howdy," he said simply. He made no offer to shake McTigue's hand, and McTigue merely nodded and smiled briefly.

"Obliged for the drink," McTigue said.

Charlie picked up his drink. "Can we sit down?" he asked Trev. "There's a lot to talk about."

He evidently was not including McTigue in this, and McTigue seemed to realize it. Trev looked at his face in the bar mirror, and the thin man was smiling faintly, sardonically.

"See you around," Trev said, and he headed for a corner table with Charlie Brackett.

"Where'd you find him?" Charlie demanded when they sat down.

"On the road," Trev said. "Just tonight. We rode in together."

"Know him?"

"I don't know him," Trev admitted.

"Bounty hunter." Charlie scowled. "Known all over this part of the country. You hadn't been away so long you'd 'a heard of him. A bad one."

Trev frowned. "Bounty hunter," he murmured.

They were the rare breed, the loners who hunted men for a price. He had no doubt now that he *had* heard McTigue's name mentioned many times at random bars. When you spoke of a bounty hunter you spoke of him with contempt that was close to hatred, and with fear, because a bounty hunter captured or killed for money. He was a man quick and deadly with a gun, and a man who had no interest in his prey except the price on his head. The price could be pretty big, too, if the hunted was wanted by a railroad company for a holdup or killing.

"He's been through here before," Charlie was saying. "Everybody knows him. When McTigue has a poster in his pocket, and he's after a man, that man had better drop dead, 'cause he'll be dead anyway."

Trev Buchman sipped his drink. "That the way McTigue brings them in?" he asked.

Charlie shrugged. "Hell," he said. "Reckon you know when a railroad or a county law officer puts up a poster for an outlaw, they'd rather have him dead than alive. He's less trouble that way. Saves a trial, an' besides, he can't get away. McTigue knows that."

Trev changed the subject. "You ride for Box B, Charlie?" he asked.

Charlie nodded. "You—you know about Jim?"

"Heard about it down in Flint Rock," Trev said, "coming north."

"From where?" Charlie asked curiously.

"Mostly Texas," Trev said. "Figured I'd like to see Jim. Got here too late."

"Hell of a thing," Charlie muttered.

"Was he sick?" Trev asked. "They said he had dizzy spells."

"His wife Ivy said he used to get 'em," Charlie explained. "Never seen him have any, myself. Hell of a way to die."

Trev fingered the glass on the table before him. "She running Box B?" he asked.

"Runs it with help from Lace Reynolds, Box B ramrod, an' from Neil Torrance."

"Don't know them," Trev said.

"Reynolds come in a few months before Jim died," Charlie explained. "Torrance is Ivy Buchman's lawyer."

Trev looked at the table. "What about Ivy Buchman?" he asked.

Charlie Brackett was a little uneasy now. "She's a looker," he said. "Easterner. Jim met her when he was East makin' a deal for some stock. Come home with her, already married. Reckon that's all anybody knows about it."

"You don't like her," Trev said.

"Hell," Charlie scowled. "Reckon I didn't say that, Trev." He added glumly, "She did come in, though, an take Box B—lock, stock an' barrel—an' she's not a Buchman."

"She's Jim's widow," Trev pointed out. "Who else could have gotten it?"

"You're Bull Buchman's son," Charlie said. "Look at it one way, an' you're entitled to it a hell of a lot more than she is."

Trev shook his head. "I didn't know Jim was dead when I started up here," he said. "Reckon I didn't come here to make trouble. Besides, if I know Jim, he left a will, and Ivy Buchman has a lawyer."

"She has a lawyer, all right," Charlie growled. "They're thicker than two peas in a pod."

Trev looked across at the little man thoughtfully. "How is Box B doing?" he asked.

"Your father built it up to the biggest spread in this part of the country," Charlie told him. "You know Jim. Jim let it slide. Bull Buchman's range took in all of the Cannon Basin. Box B has less than half of it left."

Trev whistled softly. "Nesters?" he asked, "or new ranchmen?"

"Both," Charlie said. "Pushin' in across the Cannon. Sheepherder tried to come in last week. Reynolds threw him out quick."

"Maybe Ivy Buchman will be tougher than Jim," Trev murmured. "What do you hear from Joe Fineran, Charlie?"

"Old Joe?" Charlie chuckled. "Ain't seen him in a week or two, Trev. Reckon there's a man missed you when you left here. Used to talk about you a lot."

"He all right?" Trev asked.

"All right?" Charlie repeated. "There's a man will live forever, Trev. Don't smoke, an' he don't drink. Eats them vegetables he grows. He—"

"He have any enemies around here?" Trev wanted to know. "Anybody gunning for him?"

Charlie Brackett was staring. "Gunnin' for Joe Fineran? Reckon you're crazy, Trev."

"He's dead," Trev said evenly. "Somebody got him tonight, Charlie."

Charlie Brackett pushed his chair back. "Joe Fineran? "What the hell, Trev."

"Shot him down, unarmed," Trev went on. "I stopped at his shack tonight a few minutes after they got him. He told me who did it."

"You know?" Charlie stared.

"Goes by the name of Fogarty," Trev said. "Red Fogarty."

Charlie blinked and then licked his lips.

"Know him?" Trev asked.

"Rides for Box B." Charlie muttered.

"Not any more," Trev murmured. "He's dead tonight."

Charlie was shaking his head, mystified. "Why in hell would he want to shoot Joe Fineran? Didn't think he even knew him."

"Reckon you don't have to know a man to shoot him," Trev said. "Fogarty new at Box B?"

"Reynolds brought him in," Charlie said. "Bringin' in a hell of a lot of men lately. We're carryin' near double the crew we had when Jim was runnin' the outfit."

"Where can I find this Fogarty?" Trev asked him.

"Now?" Charlie muttered.

"Right now." Trev nodded.

Charlie looked worried. "That Fogarty looked to me like he knew how to sling a gun, Trev."

"I know how to sling a gun, too," Trev murmured. "Where would he be, Charlie?"

"Maybe at Rhoda Greene's Wyoming Belle," Charlie said. "Seen him around there before."

Trev stood up. "I'm obliged for the drink, Charlie." He stopped then, and said, "Who does Fogarty run with? There were two of them."

Charlie shook his head. "Nobody in particular. . . . You sure you're doin' right, Trev? Reckon this is for the sheriff. You know Ben Walters is a good man. If Fogarty's been throwin' a long loop—"

"He killed a man tonight," Trev said patiently. "Shot him down in cold blood. Walters can't do anything about that because the only witness is Joe Fineran himself, and he's dead. I've worn a star myself, Charlie. I know what a peace officer can do and can't do. Walters can't touch this Fogarty. I can."

He started toward the door, and Charlie Brackett fell in step behind him. As they were going down along the bar past the spot where McTigue stood, the bounty hunter turned and said idly. "Got yourself another cover gun, Buchman?"

"I don't need a cover gun," Trev told him.

McTigue grinned. "My money's on you," he said. "Luck."

"Reckon I don't need that, either," Trev told him, and he passed on. Outside, he said to Charlie Brackett, "Where is the Wyoming Belle?"

"Past the hotel," Charlie told him. "You ain't thinkin' this out, Trev."

"Thinking is done," Trev said. "Time to act now. I don't want you in this, Charlie."

He walked toward the corner, preparing to cross the road to the hotel and the saloon down the street from it.

"I'm in it," Charlie said stubbornly. "Reckon you said there was two of 'em, didn't you?"

"I don't know the other one," Trev said. "Fogarty's my man. Say you don't know him well?"

"Hell," Charlie Brackett scowled. "Lace Reynolds even has this new crew in another bunkhouse from the old riders who worked for Jim. From what I can see, they ain't doin much except lookin' tough."

Trev slowed down as they came up on the walk on the other side. "Gunthrowers?" he asked slowly.

"They ain't labeled," Charlie said, "but they don't look like cowpunchers from up the creek."

Trev considered this fact as he walked in the direction of the Wyoming Belle Saloon. Fogarty rode for Box B; Lace Reynolds, Box B ramrod, had brought in another crew of loose riders who appeared to be gunslingers; tonight, Joe Fineran, a nester, squatting on Box B range for a good many years, had been shot to death. It could all add up to something, and on the other hand it could mean nothing. Possibly Fogarty had just had a grudge of some kind against poor Joe Fineran, even though this did not seem possible.

Whatever it meant, a man had died tonight, and another man would have to pay for it.

Chapter Three

THE WYOMING BELLE was one of the newer saloons in Rawdon. Trev remembered that there had been a vacant lot here when he'd left. It was not too large, but upon pushing through the batwing doors Trev immediately sensed that there was something different about this saloon.

In the first place it was clean, it was the only really clean saloon he'd ever been in as far back as he could remember. The sawdust on the floor was fresh; the spittoons and the mirrors were polished. The walls weren't dingy, and the card tables and chairs were unbattered.

The brass hanging lamps providing light in the place were bright and clean, and the three bartenders on the other side of the mahogany even wore clean aprons and had their hair plastered back neatly.

Trev remembered something, and he said suddenly, "Who did you say ran this place, Charlie?"

"Rhoda Greene," Charlie Brackett told him. "Father built it. He died two years ago. Rhoda's been runnin' it ever since. Nice gal."

Trev nodded. They stood just inside the door, and he looked over the long room. "See Fogarty?" he asked.

"Not here," Charlie told him. "Card room in the back. Reckon he could be in there, Trev. You sure—"

Trev pushed away from the door, moving down between the tables toward another door at the rear of the room. As he was stepping forward to open it, a girl came out. She wore a black satin dress with a white lace collar which made her seem almost prim in a place like this.

Her hair was coppery-red, and she had deep violet eyes. He guessed her to be about twenty-three or twenty-four. She was a fine-looking girl, on the tall side, and she stood very erect, her chin high, the mouth wide and curving.

They looked at each other for a moment at a distance of less than three feet. Trev saw the girl's face go suddenly white. Her lips started to move, and she formed the word

20

Jim with her mouth, not saying it. There was shock and almost terror in her eyes.

Behind Trev, Charlie Brackett said, "Rhoda, meet Trev Buchman, Jim's brother."

Trev nodded as he watched the girl regain her composure. She had thought she was seeing Jim Buchman come back to life, and it had had a tremendous effect upon her. There had always been a resemblance between Trev and Jim, which had sharpened with the years.

"Trev," Rhoda Greene murmured. "I've heard Jim speak of you."

"Roughest man in a free-for-all this town ever saw." Charlie Brackett grinned.

"I heard that, too," Rhoda said, looking at Trev out of those dark violet eyes.

He tried to read what was behind those eyes. Had she hoped, desperately, futilely, that it had really been Jim Buchman? And why, if Jim were a married man?

"Will you have a drink?" Rhoda invited. "The first one to a stranger is on the house."

"Had one in The Big Western," Trev said. "Reckon that'll do for now."

"You're not a heavy drinker?" She smiled.

"Work to do," Trev said, and looked past her into the room beyond, his eyes moving from table to table. There were half a dozen card tables, four of them occupied. At a fifth table a thin, round-shouldered man with bright red hair sat alone, laying cards out on the wood, solitaire-fashion. His hair was the reddest Trev had ever seen. His hat lay on the chair next to him, and the yellow light from an overhead lamp fell full across his bare head.

He had freckles to go with the hair, and narrow, slanted eyes. The face was thin and cruel, with a slit of a mouth, and a bony chin. In a way he reminded Trev of McTigue, the bounty hunter. These men were of a cast— cold-eyed killers.

Rhoda Greene was saying, "Anything wrong, Mr. Buchman?"

"We'll see," Trev murmured. He pushed past her into the room, stood just inside, and said to Charlie Brackett without looking back at him, "At that side table, alone!"

There was only one red-haired man in the place as far as he could see, but he still had to be sure.

"That's him," Charlie Brackett gulped. "Trev, you think—"

There was an empty table a few feet from the door, with several chairs around it. Trev reached forward for one of the chairs, and then pushed hard, sending it skidding across the floor and into the wall ten feet away. The chair struck with a bang and overturned. All the card games stopped. The players at the four tables looked at Trev standing just to one side of the door, one shoulder against the wall now, his thumbs hooked in his gunbelt.

"Everybody out," Trev said tonelessly, "except the redhead at the far table."

They knew what he meant, and they knew that he meant business. There was no talk. There were at least a dozen men in the room besides Fogarty. They got up and filed out into the barroom, leaving the redhead still at his table.

Fogarty hadn't gotten up. He still sat at his table, the deck of cards in his hand, counting them off, laying them out on the table. He'd glanced up when Trev had spoken, but then he'd gone on playing when the other men started to leave.

When the last man had gone through the door, Trev kicked it shut with his boot.

"Fogarty?" he said.

"Reckon you know me," Red Fogarty grinned. He had pointed white teeth and very small ears set close to his head; the lobes of the ears were pointed, too.

He wore a vest and a checked shirt, and he was armed because Trev could see the pearl handle of a Colt gun protruding just above the rim of the table. The gun was in the clear, and ready for quick use, too. This was the way men like Red Fogarty always sat—back to the wall, the gun in the clear—because death might come to them very suddenly.

"I know you," Trev said. "I knew Joe Fineran, too."

He had his man, then. Fogarty's green eyes blinked once and his head came up a little higher. He placed the deck of cards down on the table, and he rubbed his long, slender hands together. Joe Fineran had made no mistake in identifying the man who had shot him.

"Joe Fineran," Fogarty repeated softly.

"You shot down an unarmed old man tonight," Trev said softly, the anger raging through him again at the thought of it, and of the trout pools where Joe Fineran would never again cast his line. "Reckon you'd like to draw on me?"

"Fineran?" Fogarty smiled. "I don't know any Fineran, mister."

He was lying, and he knew that Trev knew it; his smile indicated as much. The lie was intended to stall for a little time because he wanted to measure his man, and he wanted to make sure that there were no odds against him. Also, if it were possible to tip the weight a little in his direction, he would do that before he drew his gun.

He sat there in his chair, body very relaxed, still smiling, but his green eyes narrowed. He was not afraid, but he wanted that little edge.

"Draw your gun," Trev said, and then he gave Red Fogarty the edge he was wanting.

He did it deliberately, wanting Fogarty to draw on him. He took a step in the direction of the door as if to place himself between the redhead and the door, and Fogarty thought to catch him while he was moving.

Trev saw his right hand leave the table, moving with incredible speed, although the rest of his body was very still. The barrel of Fogarty's Colt .45 was above the rim of the table when Trev's first bullet struck him.

Fogarty twisted sideways, an amazed expression on his face. He was hit, and hard, but he managed to get a shot off, the slug slamming into the lintel of the door above Trev's head.

A second bullet from Trev's gun caught Fogarty full in the chest, knocking him backward against the wall. He fell off the chair, and as he fell his left hand was clawing aimlessly at the cards still spread on the table, upsetting the orderly arrangement he had made.

Outside, Charlie Brackett was yelling, "Trev! You all right?"

Trev reached behind him, the gun still in his hand. He opened the door, and he said over his shoulder, "What's all the noise about, Charlie?"

He started to walk forward toward the table, and he heard a man in the doorway behind him say, "He got Red Fogarty."

Trev turned around then, and came back toward the group outside. Charlie Brackett was watching curiously, and Rhoda Greene still stood beside him.

"I suppose you had to do it," she said.

She was watching him, cold-eyed, her mouth tight.

"He had it coming," Trev told her. "From me, or someone else. His kind always has it coming."

Charlie Brackett explained it to her as he stood there, looking down at her.

"Trev says this Fogarty shot up Joe Fineran, a nester up on Squaw Creek. Fineran didn't have a gun."

"We have a law officer in Rawdon," Rhoda said quietly.

"This couldn't wait for the law, ma'am," Trev said. "He shot down a friend of mine who was unarmed. He had it coming."

"When a man sets himself up as the law," Rhoda said tersely, "and he's not wearing the star, he's asking for trouble."

"Reckon I can handle any trouble comes along," Trev told her.

A crowd of the curious from the barroom were crowding around the doorway to look in, and a man called from the street, "Lace Reynolds comin' up."

"I don't want any more trouble in here," Rhoda warned as Trev and Charlie Brackett moved toward the bar.

"I won't make it," Trev promised.

Lace Reynolds strode in through the batwing doors, a short man with tremendous shoulders, thick in the waist, thick in the legs. He had a wide, heavy-jawed face like a bulldog's, with a blunt, flattened nose and bleak gray-blue eyes.

There was something about him which reminded Trev of his own father. They walked the same way, heavy, forceful strides, the way a man walks when he's the boss and wants everybody to know he's the boss.

Reynolds walked in through the door of the back room and came out a few moments later. He said tersely, "Who did it?"

"This way," Trev called from the bar.

Lace Reynolds turned to face him, his jaw beginning to protrude a little more, and then the jaw dropped when he stared at Trev. Once again Trev realized someone was mistaking him for his brother.

Charlie Brackett corrected the mistake immediately. "Jim Buchman's brother," Charlie said. "Just rode into town, Reynolds."

Lace Reynolds came up to them slowly. "Reckon you

didn't waste much time." He scowled. "You know Fogarty before you got here?"

"Never saw him until five minutes ago," Trev stated.

Reynolds stared at him. "You're damned quick with that gun, mister," he said peevishly. "What in hell did you have against Fogarty?"

"He shot up Joe Fineran," Trev told him. "Fineran was a friend of mine."

He watched Reynolds' face closely as he said this, wondering if Fogarty had gone down to Squaw Creek on Reynolds' instructions. The Box B foreman's face showed nothing. He still didn't like what had happened, not because Fogarty had been a friend of his, but because Fogarty had ridden for him, and one of his riders getting the worst of a gun duel was in a sense a reflection upon him.

"Why in hell would Fogarty shoot up a nester like Fineran?" Reynolds demanded.

"Ask Fogarty," Trev countered.

"You got proof Fogarty shot him?"

"Fineran told me," Trev stated, "before he died. That good enough for you?"

He was asking Reynolds to say he was a liar, and Lace Reynolds seemed to sense this, and he resented it. Trev wondered, idly, what attitude Reynolds would have taken if he, Trev Buchman, were not the brother-in-law of the Box B owner.

"You're sayin' it," Reynolds growled. He wasn't committing himself either way. "I'll tell Mrs. Buchman you're in town," he said, and he turned and left the saloon.

He passed Sheriff Ben Walters coming in, Trev remembered Ben well. Walters, now eight years older, was graying, and his shoulders seemed to be a little more stooped, but his eyes were as clear as ever, and he walked with a steady step. Trev figured him to be in his late fifties now, a tall man, solidly built, not a handsome man —his nose was too big and his ears protruded—but Trev remembered him as a good man who'd tried always to keep the rough young ones in line and still give them a measure of liberty.

Ben Walters had already heard who'd done the killing, and when he came in he looked at Trev, nodded impersonally, and went into the back room.

When he came out and headed for the bar, Rhoda

Greene had signaled for a bartender to bring up two drinks. They were waiting for Trev and Ben Walters when the sheriff of Rawdon came up.

"Obliged, Rhoda." Ben nodded as he picked up his glass.

"How's it, Ben," Trev murmured.

Ben Walters tilted the glass in Trev's direction. "Reckon you didn't waste any time," he said. "How long you been in Rawdon?"

Trev figured the time. "Half hour," he said. "Little more; little less."

Charlie Brackett was still at Trev's elbow, and Ben Walters said to him, "Take a walk, Charlie."

"Hell!" Charlie scowled. "Trev just came in."

"See him tomorrow," Ben told him.

Charlie moved away, but Trev noticed that Rhoda Greene was lingering nearby, on the other side of the bar now, talking with a customer, but occasionally glancing in his direction.

"So you shot a man," Ben murmured after he'd downed his drink. "When you were here before you just worked on them with your fists."

"This one needed shooting," Trev observed. "Reckon he wasn't the kind would take fists anyway, Ben. You know his kind."

"Maybe I know your kind, too," Ben said grimly.

Trev looked at him steadily. "I worked as a law man down in Texas," he said quietly, "and as a range detective. I've been on the good side, Ben, on your side."

Ben Walters rubbed his jaw reflectively. He said apologetically, "When you left here, Trev, I figured you'd go one way or the other. Nobody knew, then. When I heard you'd shot up Red Fogarty I figured you'd gone with the wild bunch. You tell me I figured wrong and I believe you. The Buchmans never lie."

"Fogarty had it coming," Trev said.

"Why?" Ben asked.

Trev gave him the details of his evening ride into Rawdon tonight. Walters listened carefully, saying nothing until Trev had finished. Then, "Joe Fineran never told you why Fogarty had come for him?"

"Died before he could," Trev said. "Fineran knew, and right before Fogarty pulled his gun on me, I knew, too."

Ben Walters frowned. "Hell of a business," he said slowly. "Didn't even know Fogarty knew Joe Fineran."

"He's new in this town?"

"Few months," Walters said.

Trev fingered his glass on the bar. "Charlie Brackett tells me Reynolds has more like Fogarty on his payroll. Why?"

"Damned if I know," Walters confessed. "Lace has a pretty big crew out at Box B now. That's all I know about it." He looked at Trev curiously, then he said, "What brings you back to Rawdon, Trev?"

Trev shrugged. "Figured I'd stop by and see Jim. I got here too late."

"You staying now?"

Trev looked at him. "Any reason why I should stay?" he said.

Ben Walters frowned again. "Jim's dead," he said. "There was a will, and it's all cut and dried. Ivy Buchman owns Box B."

"I didn't come here for anything," Trev reminded him. "I didn't know Jim was dead when I came north."

"You figure on seeing her?"

Trev nodded. "She was Jim's wife," he said. "I'll have to ride by and pay my respects."

Ben Walters didn't say anything to that, and Trev said to him quietly, "What do you think of her, Ben?"

Ben's mouth tightened imperceptibly. He was glancing over in Rhoda Greene's direction when he said, "Reckon Jim could have done better, Trev."

Trev had it out in the open, then; he'd been wondering about it ever since he'd met Rhoda. Ben Walters was a good judge of human nature; he'd seen enough men to be able to distinguish between the good and the bad, and Ben believed that Ivy Buchman had not been good for Jim.

"Jim and Rhoda Greene pretty good friends?" Trev asked.

Ben looked at him. "They used to go around some," he stated. "Not my business, Trev, but I had it figured Jim would marry Rhoda. Kind of surprised me when he came back here with a wife."

"Over the hill and gone," Trev murmured, and he wondered if it really was. A girl who had not been good for Jim now owned all of Box B, the largest ranch in Cannon Basin, and that was the end of it, only it would have been much nicer if she and Jim had gotten along. There was, also, Charlie Brackett's remark that Ivy Buchman and her lawyer, Neil Torrance, were closer than peas in a pod, and this only a matter of weeks after Jim had died—by accident.

Accident, Trev thought slowly. He still couldn't conceive of Jim falling off a corral fence, dizzy spell or no dizzy spell.

Chapter Four

EARLY IN THE MORNING Trev came down from his room at the Drovers Hotel to find McTigue, the bounty hunter, sitting on the porch, smoking a cigar, his boots up on the porch rail.

He'd known that McTigue was staying at the Drovers because when he himself had registered, after seeing Ben Walters, he'd noticed McTigue's name just above his own on the registry book.

McTigue glanced back at him, smiled, and said, "Hear you did pretty well last night. Reckon you didn't need that cover gun."

"I didn't need it," Trev said.

McTigue took the cigar from his mouth and looked at it. "Made any plans," he asked, "now that you're back home?"

"Why?" Trev asked him.

McTigue shrugged. "Figured you might be ridin' out to Box B," he said. "I might like to tail along."

Trev shook his head. "Not with me," he stated. "Where you go, McTigue, you're not welcome."

McTigue's grin broadened. "Where you're going," he asked softly, "are you?"

Trev looked at him. "Who are you after in this town?" he asked.

"Maybe you." McTigue laughed. "Look at it this way, Buchman. A man in your position could always use a cover gun."

"What's my position?" Trev asked him.

McTigue flipped his cigar butt out into the road. "You ride into Rawdon and you kill a man," he said. "You kill a man who rides for Box B, which is a spread a lot of people around here might figure rightfully belongs to you. The man you shot up was a rider for Lace Reynolds, ramrod for Box B. Why should either Reynolds, or this woman, be glad to see you around?"

"Why should you want to help me?" Trev countered.

"Maybe I like your style." McTigue grinned. "Maybe

29

with you I have a reason for being here, and maybe two guns are always better than one, no matter what your business."

"I don't like your business," Trev told him flatly.

"When you make a deal for a gun," McTigue chuckled, you don't have to like the gun. You just know that it's what you need. With it you might live a little longer. Without it—" He stopped and shrugged, looking at Trev questioningly.

"Reckon you got the wrong man," Trev growled, and went down the porch steps and across the road to a restaurant to have his breakfast.

An hour later he was astride the gray gelding again and riding west out of Rawdon. He'd met a few people this morning who knew him and had stopped to talk with him, and in their eyes, although they had not said it, he read the sympathy. Not too many people had loved Bull Buchman, but Trev had had his friends in this town, and all of them thought Box B should have gone to a Buchman, not to a stranger.

Pushing out into Cannon Basin, he was in home territory. He remembered these low hills with the ridge of mountains rising up abruptly on the other side of the Cannon River. To the north the Catamount Mountains hemmed in the basin, and the Yellow Hills, low, bleak and barren, a refuge for cattle rustlers, formed the south boundary.

Leaving Rawdon, the land rose gradually, falling only when it neared the Cannon River a dozen miles to the west. Trev followed the well-defined road which led out to Box B, remembering how many hundred times he'd ridden this when he was younger. For the first time he was almost glad that he was home, even though it was for only a brief stay, and the home was no longer his.

Also for the first time, he experienced a slight resentment over the fact that Ivy Buchman, and not himself, owned Box B. He knew that this was foolishness: he'd left without his father's blessings, and he deserved nothing. But this girl had married into the estate which he and Jim, when younger, had worked hard with their father to build.

He told himself that he was being foolish; that he should pay his respects to Ivy Buchman, and then ride out of here. He had some money in his pockets, and he was young, and he could always find work. There was a job waiting for him back in Texas if he wanted it as range detective for a cattlemen's association, and there were always towns in the West where an experienced peace officer with a reference would be most welcome.

Cannon Basin was home, though, and there were memories here, and he'd discovered that he still had friends here. Rhoda Greene might become an added inducement. She was a strikingly fine-looking girl, and she'd liked Jim before he'd married Ivy. If he stayed here long enough . . .

He was in the middle of this reverie when a rifle cracked, and a bullet whipped past his head. He reacted instinctively, not even looking in the direction from which the bullet had come, or attempting to draw his gun. He was out in the open here, and the shot had come from a low hill to his left about a hundred and fifty yards distant.

His first move was to get out of range of a second shot —the first had been uncomfortably close. The gray responded beautifully by surging ahead at a full gallop.

Trev bent low in the saddle, leaning his body to the far side of the horse away from the rifleman on the hill. He expected another shot before he was able to get around a thick stand of pine at the base of another low hill, but the shot didn't come.

When he was out of sight around the timber, he swung from the saddle, slapped the gray to keep the animal moving, and then ran hard, working his way around the base of this second hill in the direction of the hill from which the shot had come.

He had his bearings now, and he remembered this place well. An old schoolhouse had once stood on the grade from which the shot had come, and as a boy he'd played around the still remaining foundation. The rifleman had undoubtedly been concealed in this hiding place.

Trev came up on the hill from the rear. As he climbed carefully he could still hear the gray running in the distance. The rifleman in the hole would be hearing the same thing and thinking that the rider was still with the horse.

Slipping the Colt gun from the holster, Trev approached the summit of the hill, making sure not to dislodge any stones or pebbles which would warn his man that he was approaching. He was working on the assumption now that

the bushwhacker had waylayed him to avenge the death of
Red Fogarty—he might even be Fogarty's accomplice the
previous night when Fineran had been killed.

Down the grade behind him he could see a horse tied at
the edge of a clump of ash, which meant that the man
was still here. Trev was within a few yards of the brow of
the hill now, and he deliberated for a moment whether to
inch forward or make those last few yards in several long
leaps which would bring him right up to the hole, gun in
hand.

He decided upon the latter course in view of the fact
that the killer would be leaving his ambush at any moment and might surprise Trev while he was still flat on
the ground, unable to get off an advantageous shot.

Gripping the gun, Trev rushed forward, making no
attempt at quiet now. He came up on the rim of the
foundation wall, his gun seeking the target, but the hole
on the hill was empty.

He stared, uncomprehending, remembering the horse
still tied at the base of the hill, and then a voice drifted
across the fifteen-foot-wide hole: "Drop the gun, Buchman."

He saw a rifle barrel protruding over the edge of a
rock, the muzzle of the gun pointing straight at him. It
was very steady. He could see only the top of a man's hat
above the rock, and the target was very small. He would
have taken the risk, but he was positive he wasn't going
to be killed now. The man behind that rifle had had him
covered all the while and could have killed him at any-
time, if he'd wanted to.

Trev dropped the gun at his feet, close enough so that
if the killer did open up on him now, there was the bare
possibility that he could fall on the gun and get off a shot
or two before he died.

The rifle barrel dropped and the man behind the rock
sat up, grinning. Trev knew now why the voice had had a
strangely familiar ring to it. The man getting up to his
feet was McTigue, the bounty hunter.

"Pick up your gun, Buchman." McTigue chuckled.
"Couldn't risk your throwin' lead at me before you
knew who it was."

A glint in his gray eyes, Trev picked up the gun and
slipped it back into the holster.

"What in hell is to stop me from throwing lead now?"

he snapped. "You put a bullet damned close to my head down there."

"You think," McTigue asked softly, "it couldn't have come closer if I'd wanted?" He added dryly, "Could have picked you off ever since you left the trees below an' started climbin' up here. You were right out in the open, mister. That damn horse trick didn't fool me. I've seen all the tricks, an' I got a few of my own nobody's ever seen."

Trev could well believe this after the little encounter with the bounty hunter. He said tersely, "What was this for?"

"Still figure you can get along without a cover gun?" McTigue smiled. "You'd have been dead, Buchman, if it was somebody else."

"If a man's out to bushwhack me," Trev growled, "and he wants to do it badly enough, what's to stop him?"

"Me," McTigue murmured, "if you'll work it the same way on my side of the fence."

"To hell with you," Trev snapped, "and your side of the fence."

He turned and strode down the hill, angered by this strange man and his peculiar method of lining up friends for himself. He wondered if McTigue always operated in this manner, forming alliances with quick-trigger men who needed an extra gun as much as he did.

Several hundred yards up the trace he found the gray waiting for him. He stepped into the saddle and rode on toward Box B, which was on the west side of the basin.

He was anxious now to meet Ivy Buchman, having heard so much talk about her. This was the girl who had won the affections of Jim from Rhoda Greene, who was not hard to look at, either, and who had apparently either loved Jim, or been very close to it. . . .

It was high noon when Trev topped the last low rise and saw Box B spread out before him along the east bank of the Cannon. The ranch house itself was not too big because Bull Buchman had never believed in comfort for himself or for his help, but there was quite a number of outbuildings, stables, solid pole corrals.

The cottonwoods around the house, which had been small when Trev left, were now of a fairly good size. The house was low and long, of rough-sawed boards, which Bull Buchman had had hauled down from the Catamount

Mountains. A veranda occupied the entire south side, and a new wing had been built along the west side. There were a few flowers planted here and there, which Bull Buchman would have despised.

A rider was swinging in across the meadow beyond the house, driving half a dozen horses, and even from the distance Trev recognized little Charlie Brackett.

He rode down the trace, passing one of the corrals, and then a bunkhouse which was new to him. A man came out of the bunkhouse to look at him as he went by. He didn't like the looks of the man; he wore his gun low, and his clothes were too clean and in too good condition for a common rider. This was a man who, like Fogarty, had been hired not for his ability to work stock, but for another purpose.

Charlie Brackett had stated that Box B carried practically two crews now, and one of them seemed to be doing little work, even bunking separately from the work crew.

The corner of the main house that had been used as Bull Buchman's office had a door which faced the main bunkhouse. Lace Reynolds was coming out of this door as Trev rode up and dismounted.

Reynolds stopped to look at him, and then he nodded coldly and went on down to the bunkhouse. After tying the gray to the hitchrail in front of the house, Trev walked around to the front. It was strange to be here again. This had been his home; he'd been born here, he'd played here as a child, and then he'd worked here with his father and his brother. And now both were gone, and a strange girl he'd never seen owned and occupied the house.

He heard a door open as he came up on the veranda, and then a girl came out. She'd evidently been expecting him, and possibly she'd seen him riding down the trace.

She was younger than he'd anticipated, probably not more than twenty-one or twenty-two, with tawny hair, a full, rich mouth, and perfectly shaped nose. She wore a white blouse and tight-fitting, fawn-colored riding pants with brown boots. Her eyes were a peculiar shade of amber, matching her hair perfectly.

She was not as tall as Rhoda Greene, but she *was* a looker, and she would attract men. She was smiling as Trev came up, revealing perfectly matched white teeth, small and even, and she held out a small, brown hand.

"You're Trev," she said. "Jim has told me about you. I'm glad you came out."

"Didn't hear the news," Trev told her, "until I was at Flint Rock."

He shook her hand, finding it warm and firm, and noticed that she held his hand a little longer than was necessary, and he was not anxious to have her take it away. He understood now why Jim had fallen for her.

"You look like Jim," Ivy Buchman was saying. "I'm glad you came out. Lace told me you were in town."

"He tell you everything?" Trev asked.

"About our rider?" Ivy asked. "That was too bad, your first night in town. Lace still has no idea why Fogarty shot the man."

"Has he tried to find out?" Trev wanted to know.

"He's made some inquiries in the bunkhouse," Ivy said almost carelessly. "Fogarty was a new man, and not too well known. It undoubtedly was a private quarrel."

"If Fineran had been armed," Trev stated, "I might have stayed out of it."

"You knew Fineran pretty well?"

"Since I was a boy," Trev told her. "He was a harmless old man."

Ivy Buchman deftly changed the subject. "I'm having lunch in a few minutes," she invited. "Will you join me, Trev?"

"My pleasure . . . sister," he murmured, and he saw the grin come to her face.

The interior of the house was quite tastefully furnished. When Trev had lived here, the motherless house had been quite barren, but Ivy had brought in new eastern furniture, lamps, soft rugs and filmy curtains.

An Indian woman served them in the dining room. The food was tastefully prepared, undoubtedly under Ivy's directions.

Over the meal Trev asked a few brief questions concerning Jim. Ivy, as far as he could see, was not in mourning, and Jim's death had not been a particularly hard blow for her. She was in good spirits.

"I miss Jim," she admitted, "but he was not in good health, Trev. He'd been having these dizzy spells. Several times I urged him to see Doc Waterbury in town, but he put it off."

Trev didn't say anything to this. He remembered Jim

only as strong and healthy as himself, and it seemed foolish of him not to have gone to the doctor when these spells had come on.

"What are your plans, Trev?" Ivy wanted to know.

She was leaning across the table, and Trev felt himself being drawn toward her in spite of himself. He'd already gauged her as a woman who liked to have a lot of men around her. According to Charlie Brackett she already had the lawyer Torrance chasing at her heels. A woman with her looks would always have men, and she could drop them as easily as she picked them up.

"Figured I'd see you," Trev murmured, "and then ride on."

"This is your home," Ivy told him. "In a way I hate to be taking it from you."

Trev shrugged. "It was Jim's," he said. "I was out of this years ago. Jim fell into harness better than I did."

"You could still stay here," Ivy told him.

Trev looked at her.

"I don't mean in the house, of course." She smiled. "At Box B. We always could use more men." She was watching his face closely now. "I don't mean as a rider."

"What do you mean?" Trev wanted to know.

"I can't drop Reynolds as foreman," Ivy said, "but you could work with him in running Box B. You know cattle, and you've worked this ranch before."

Trev wondered why she couldn't drop Reynolds if she wanted to. He said, "Haven't made any plans, yet."

"Please think it over, Trev," she urged.

Trev Buchman wondered if he would be a fool not to. Box B, even having lost half its range land, was still the biggest spread in the Cannon Basin, and Ivy Buchman apparently was impressed by him. She was young and single now, and undoubtedly she would again marry. Why not him?

He looked at her across the table. "I'll think it over," he promised.

He had the strange feeling, though, that this was not all of Ivy Buchman sitting opposite him. He was seeing her better half; the other half was not here.

Chapter Five

THEY WERE BOTH out at one of the corrals after having eaten, looking over some high-grade Morgan horses Jim had bought a short while before his death, when a buckboard came down the trace.

Ivy said, "You haven't met Mr. Torrance, my lawyer?"

"Not yet," Trev told her.

He watched the buckboard coming up. A man in a tan coat and brown Stetson sat on the seat.

"Neil has been very helpful," Ivy stated, "handling all the legal ends of the estate."

"Nice having friends," Trev murmured. He thought that Ivy looked at him rather sharply.

Torrance stepped down from the buckboard and came toward them, smiling. He was as big as Trev, and about the same age, a fine-looking man, chestnut hair, brown eyes. His handshake was strong when Ivy introduced them.

"Wanted to meet Jim's brother." Torrance smiled.

"You knew Jim?" Trev asked.

"We've done a little business together." Torrance nodded. "I'm new to this town, also, and I never got to know him well."

"I've been trying to persuade Trev to take a job at Box B," Ivy said.

Trev watched Neil Torrance's face when Ivy said this, and although the reaction was very slight, he caught it. Torrance did not approve of this idea, and he was annoyed with Ivy for having made the proposal. He still smiled, though, and he said, "Box B could use a few good men, I'm sure, Mrs. Buchman."

Trev Buchman made up his mind quite suddenly. There were a number of things he didn't like about the setup at Box B. Torrance didn't want him around to begin with, and Torrance was quite friendly with Ivy Buchman. Jim's death had been sudden and very peculiar. Lace Reynolds had a crew of loose riders with him on Box B, and one of them had shot up Joe Fineran; the others were here for a purpose. There were too many loose ends which

37

should have been tied up, and it would be foolish of him just to ride off and forget the whole business. Jim had been his brother; Bull Buchman, who'd fought and sweated for what he had in Cannon Basin, had been his father. To both of them he owed something—at least satisfaction in his own mind that Jim's death had been natural and that Ivy Buchman rightfully deserved Box B.

"Reckon I'll take the job," he said to Ivy, and this time Neil Torrance's jaw dropped a little, and there was definite anger and resentment in his brown eyes for one brief moment.

Then he was smiling again, and Ivy said, "We can use you, Trev. I'll talk to Lace right away. How soon can you get out here?"

"Have a few things at the hotel in town," Trev told her. "I could be back in the morning." He paused, and then added, "I'm not looking for special favors as a relative," he said. "I'll live at the bunkhouse with the other men, and I'll take my orders from Reynolds."

Neil Torrance said, "You couldn't very well drop Reynolds, Mrs. Buchman, could you?"

This time Ivy Buchman looked at him, her amber eyes sharp and narrow. Torrance had touched on a sore spot here, and he knew it, and he'd said it for that reason, and some of the tigress in Ivy Buchman was showing now.

"I had no intention of dropping Reynolds," she said flatly.

Again, Trev Buchman wondered why. Who was Lace Reynolds that he could not be fired if Ivy wanted a new ramrod for Box B?

"You won't be taking orders from Reynolds," Ivy said to Trev. "I'll make an arrangement with him. I think you can be handling the stock, and Lace can . . . can take care of the business angles."

Trev had never known before that there was enough business to keep a ranch foreman so busy that he didn't have time to handle his stock and the crew that worked it as well.

Neil Torrance was still at the corral with Ivy when Trev walked down to the bunkhouse for a chat with Charlie Brackett before heading back to Rawdon. The little puncher was overjoyed when he learned that Trev was back with Box B.

"Didn't figure she'd want to sign you on, Trev." Charlie grinned.

"Torrance didn't seem so anxious," Trev observed. "Where does he fit in here?"

"Damned if I know," Charlie told him.

"And why can't Lace Reynolds be let go," Trev asked, "if Ivy Buchman wanted to sign me as ramrod?"

"You ask a hell of a lot of questions." Charlie smiled. "Now I'll ask you one. How did Jim Buchman fall into a corral an' get himself stepped on?"

"You here when it happened?"

"Nobody seen it happen," Charlie growled. "Lace had the whole damn crew out workin' the stock. We come back an' it was all over. Lace says he seen him sittin' up there on the corral fence. Half-hour later they found him dead."

Trev hadn't known that Lace Reynolds had been the last man to see Jim alive. It was something he would have to file in the back of his mind and remember.

Charlie Brackett was saying, "You just walk easy with that crowd up at the other bunkhouse, Trev. Reckon they ain't gonna take too kindly to you on account of your shootin' up Red Fogarty."

"I'll watch them."

Trev rode off a few minutes later, and as he passed the house he saw Ivy Buchman and Neil Torrance sitting on the veranda. Ivy waved a hand to him as he went by.

He wondered now as he rode back toward Rawdon if he had done the right thing. He'd had no intention of remaining here after learning of Jim's death, but something had been pushing him. There were questions somebody had to answer, and he could learn the answers only by staying here.

Riding back to town he wondered if he'd run into Mc-Tigue again, but he met only Rhoda Greene, owner of the Wyoming Belle. He met her after he'd left the trace and taken a short cut over a ridge and across a small stream known as the Anchor.

Rhoda was riding a fine sorrel horse. She was preparing to dismount and water the sorrel at the stream when Trev rode up on her. She was hatless and her copper-colored hair caught the rays of the sun. She wore a gray flannel shirt and worn blue Levis.

Trev slowed down and watched her as she walked the horse down to the water's edge.

"Out for the exercise?" he asked.

"I ride quite often," she told him. "I like to get the beer smell out of my nostrils."

"Then why are you operating a saloon?" Trev asked curiously.

"You want me to sew clothes?" She smiled. "The Wyoming belonged to my father. I fell into it." She watched him as he dismounted and let the gray drink at the stream. "You've been visiting," she said.

"I met my sister-in-law." Trev nodded.

"She's quite beautiful, isn't she?"

"She is beautiful," Trev nodded again. "She offered me a job at Box B. I'm to help Lace Reynolds run the stock."

He saw the disappointment in Rhoda Greene's dark eyes, and he knew what she was thinking. He had fallen for Ivy's charms just as Jim had.

"I—I didn't think you'd be staying," Rhoda murmured.

"Some things I have to find out," Trev told her. "You knew Jim pretty well Ben Walters tells me you used to go around with him."

"We went to the dances in town on occasion," Rhoda said. "I liked Jim."

"What about those sick spells he was supposed to have. You ever see him get dizzy?"

"I never saw it," Rhoda said quietly. "Of course this could have developed after he married Mrs. Buchman."

"You didn't like Ivy," Trev said.

Rhoda's head came up. "Was I supposed to like her?" she demanded. "Do you want me to be a hypocrite? Jim and I had been pretty good friends. He went East and he came back with a wife. I didn't like it. That's your answer. I don't like her, either."

Trev smiled faintly. "It's straight enough," he murmured, and he liked this girl for her honesty. "You going into town? I'll ride back with you."

"Your boss mightn't like it," Rhoda said grimly.

"She's paying me to run her stock," Trev observed.

Rhoda Greene just smiled at him. "You'll find out," she said.

They rode back to Rawdon together. . . .

Coming into town, Trev saw McTigue sitting on the

porch of the hotel as they went by. McTigue touched his hat to them and smiled.

"You know him?" Trev asked.

"Everybody knows about him," Rhoda said. "He's not well liked."

When they pulled up in front of the Wyoming Belle she said, "Will you have a drink? It's on the house for seeing me home."

"I'm obliged," Trev said.

He stepped into the almost empty saloon with her, and she signaled for the bartender to bring him a drink. He noticed that she herself didn't drink.

"When do you start work at Box B?" she asked.

"Riding out tomorrow," Trev told her.

"I'd be careful."

"Why?" Trev asked as he fingered the glass on the wood in front of him.

"I don't like that crew Reynolds has riding for him. I didn't like Fogarty who used to come in here. Why does Ivy Buchman need gunthrowers on her payroll?"

"You know they're gunthrowers?" Trev asked.

"What do you think?" she challenged.

Trev had no more to say on the subject. Fogarty had been a killer, not a range rider. Those men who lived at the second bunkhouse at Box B were gunslingers according to Charlie Brackett, too.

"I'll be careful," Trev promised, and he wondered why she was concerned.

"You remind me of Jim," she said as if reading his thoughts, "only you're a lot tougher, but they can stop you, too."

"The way they stopped Jim?" Trev asked softly.

"I didn't say that," she murmured, and that was all he could get out of her.

Back at the hotel, McTigue was still sitting in the same position on the porch, and as Trev went past him, the bounty hunter said softly. "So you signed up with her."

Trev paused. "How did you know?" he asked.

"Figured it out." McTigue grinned. "Reckon I know your style, mister. You wouldn't ride away from a thing like this. You're stayin', and my offer still stands. "You could use another gun."

"Who are you after?" Trev asked him.

"Who are you after?" McTigue smiled.

Trev just looked at him, and then went up to his room. . . .

Later on in the afternoon he saw Neil Torrance riding back into town in the buckboard. Torrance had an office a few doors down from the hotel. Trev had noticed it when he'd gone out to eat that morning. He watched Torrance turn the buckboard into a livery stable across from his office and then come out a few minutes after and step into the office. . . .

Ben Walters stopped in to see Trev that evening just before suppertime. The sheriff of Rawdon tilted his chair back against the wall, pushed his hat back on his head, and said thoughtfully, "So you figured you'd stay a while, Trev."

"A while." Trev nodded.

"She change your mind?"

Trev looked at him. "Reckon I made up my own mind," he stated. He watched Ben Walters frowning at the floor a moment, and then he said, "You been out to Joe Fineran's place?"

"I rode out," Ben nodded. "Still can't figure what made this Fogarty chap draw a gun on poor Joe."

"This might just be the beginning of it," Trev told him.

"Of what?" Ben asked.

"Reckon we'll just watch and see," Trev said. "This has been a quiet town for a long time, Ben."

"I've been lucky." The older man smiled grimly. "How long can you be lucky?"

Trev Buchman didn't know, but that night he began to wonder if his own luck had not run out.

Chapter Six

Trev was eating alone when Charlie Brackett burst into the hotel dining room with word that half a dozen of Lace Reynolds' gunsharps were riding into Rawdon. He'd overheard one of them say they had a little business to finish with the hombre who'd shot up Red Fogarty.

Charlie was all excited as he sat opposite Trev at the table, watching Trev finish his steak.

"They figure on gangin' up on you, Trev." He scowled. "If I was you I'd get the hell out of town for the night."

"Have to ride out to Box B tomorrow," Trev reminded him. "That's where they're holed up. I'll run into them sooner or later."

"There's six," Charlie spluttered. "You ain't standin' up against six, Trev?"

Trev shrugged as he calmly went on eating. He said to the girl who was waiting on him, "I'd like another cup of coffee."

"Coffee!" Charlie growled. "Hells bells, Trev!"

"Have a cup with me," Trev invited.

"You're plumb crazy," Charlie snapped. "I'm gettin' Ben Walters over here."

Trev looked at him. "I'm not asking for protection," he said. "Stay where you are, Charlie."

Charlie fretted and stormed up and down the room, and then went out on the porch. As Trev was finishing his second cup of coffee, Charlie came in with the news that the Box B riders were coming in.

Trev saw them ride past the window where he sat eating. There were six of them, lean, hawk-faced men. Trev was remembering that one of these men had undoubtedly been with Fogarty up at Squaw Creek the night Joe Fineran was shot, and possibly he'd had his gun on Joe, too. Trev Buchman owed that man something, also.

"Headin' down toward the Wyomin' Belle," Charlie said tersely, watching them from the window. "You just sit tight an' let 'em wonder where in hell you are. They come lookin' for you, an' it's a job for Ben Walters."

43

Trev didn't say anything about this. He finished his coffee, paid for the meal, and then went out on the porch. For once he didn't see McTigue, the bounty hunter, around.

Charlie Brackett trailed out after him, watching him light up a cigar and then take a seat in one of the chairs on the porch.

"What are you figurin' on doin'?" Charlie demanded.

"Smoke this cigar," Trev told him. He put his boots up on the porch rail and looked down the street toward the Wyoming Belle where at least a dozen horses were drawn up at the tie rail.

"All right," Charlie growled. "All right. Just stay away from there. Smoke your cigar."

"When I'm ready to go down," Trev told him, "I'll go down."

"You're crazy!" Charlie exploded, then turned and left at a run.

Trev only smiled. He'd killed a man, and some of this man's friends wanted a showdown. He had to give it to them sooner or later, or ride away from this place. He wasn't figuring on riding away until he was ready to ride, so he had no choice but to see them. Unlike Charlie Brackett, he didn't think Reynolds' gunslingers would gang up on him. These men were wolves, but they were lone wolves, and they had their pride in their profession. They would come at him one at a time if it came to a fight. They would be curious now about this man who had outdrawn one of their number.

The night came very quickly to Rawdon. The sun dropped behind the ridges on the other side of the Cannon River and shadows filled the streets. Yellow lamplight illumined the windows, and more people were seen in the street as the coolness came. Riders drifted in from other ranches in the basin, and then Rhoda Greene came up on the porch of the hotel. Trev said to her, "Looking for me?"

She came over to him in the shadows. "There are riders from Box B at my place," she said. "They're friends of Fogarty, and one of them asked for you."

"Reckon I'll have to see him," Trev murmured.

"They came out to kill you," Rhoda said.

"We don't know that," Trev told her. "You just think that."

"You *know* it."

Trev walked out to the edge of the porch and stood there for a moment. He saw Charlie Brackett and Ben Walter hurrying toward him from the direction of the sheriff's office, and he was a little amused at Charlie's concern for him.

Walters said when he came up, "What is this, Trev?"

"Plenty of smoke," Trev smiled. "No fire as yet."

"There'll be a hell of a big fire," Charlie growled, "if you go down to the Wyoming Belle."

Walters said to Rhoda Greene, "It's true about the Box B riders down there?"

"They're looking for him," Rhoda nodded toward Trev.

Trev said, "Reckon you can't stop me from going down, Ben."

"I can't stop you," Ben told him. "All I can give you is advice. Don't go down."

Trev said to Rhoda Greene, "You sell liquor at your place?"

"I sell liquor." She nodded.

"Reckon I'll have a drink." Trev smiled and went down to the walk in the direction of the Wyoming Belle.

When he reached the corner, a man stepped out from the shadows and fell in step beside him.

"Nice night for a walk," McTigue said.

"Walk the other way," Trev told him.

"Figured I'd have a drink at the Wyoming Belle, too." McTigue grinned. "Any objections?"

"Drink where you damn please." Trev scowled.

They passed the half-dozen Box B horses at the tie rack and went up on the walk. Trev glanced back once and saw Rhoda Greene, Charlie Brackett and Ben Walters coming along behind him.

McTigue saw them too, and said, "Man can't even set himself up to die without a whole flock of friends there to see him off."

"I don't figure on dying," Trev said.

"Don't figure you will." McTigue smiled.

He followed Trev into the saloon, which was fairly crowded, and Trev immediately spotted the six Box B riders at the bar. He recognized one of them, having seen him at the ranch; the others he knew almost from instinct—they were a race set apart. There was an air of insolence about them which other men lacked. These

were men who fancied themselves lords of the earth
because they were quick and deadly with the six-gun.
Trev had seen them in Texas and in other states. One
physical characteristic labeled them all. They were lean
men. He had never run across a fat man who was a
killer.

Trev moved up to the bar. He saw the six Box B men
turn to look at him, to measure him. They looked at
McTigue, too, and they knew him, and they were curious.

"You drinkin'?" McTigue asked Trev.

"No," Trev said.

McTigue was smiling, but there was a change in the
man now. He was a killer in a different field, and he
smelled blood, and now he was one of them because
he, too, was quick with the gun. He seemed to be sniffing
with his sharp nose, and his eyes, which were a peculiar
shade of light brown, seemed to be turning yellowish
in color.

"You didn't came here to drink?" McTigue said loudly,
so that all of the men along the bar could hear him.
"What brings you here, Buchman?"

Trev understood him now. He was pushing this thing
deliberately, possibly because he wanted to force Trev
to depend upon him and thus make him an unwilling
ally, but more likely because killing was in his blood. It
was a fever with him, and even the odds meant nothing,
and numbers meant nothing.

Trev said evenly, "Somebody looking for me here,
McTigue."

He had a look at them in the bar mirror then, and
although they concealed their inner feelings admirably, he
was sure he'd surprised them. They'd expected to have
to hunt for him in this town, and here he'd deliberately
sought them out, one against six. They still didn't know
about McTigue. They knew the bounty hunter as a bad
man with a six-gun. They still didn't know which side
he was on.

The second man down from Trev pulled back from the
bar and sat down on the edge of an empty table nearby.

"You Buchman?" he asked.

Trev faced him. "You know me," he said.

McTigue pulled away from Trev. He stepped back
about half a dozen paces and said softly, "Everybody

else is out of it. Reckon you boys know I mean what I say."

Nobody moved at the bar. Trev stood there facing the man who sat on the edge of the table. He was younger than the others, blond-haired, green-eyed, his nose smashed across the bridge. He wore a brown leather vest, and the gun on his hip was a Navy Colt, a big gun, tied to his leg with a leather thong.

A man down at the far end of the bar said thoughtfully, "Reckon Langham is enough for him, boys."

Langham was grinning as he sat on the table, and his gun was clear, ready for action.

"You want anything?" Trev asked him.

"You," Langham smiled. "Just you, Buchman."

He had even white teeth, and he was a nice-looking boy, but there was that coldness in his eyes now which made him almost less than human. He was an animal ready to kill.

Rhoda Greene walked in, then, with Ben Walters and Charlie Brackett. Rhoda said flatly, "That's it, boys. Lights out. We're closed for the night."

There weren't too many men in the Wyoming Belle now because most of them had started to move out through the front door and the rear-room door when they saw what the setup was.

The two bartenders behind the bar, hearing Rhoda's voice, came into sight, and at a signal from her, one of them started turning out the lamps.

Langham laughed. "Reckon that won't do any good, Miss Greene," he said.

"You Box B men know what's good for you," Ben Walters said grimly, "you'll ride out of town."

Young Langham was looking straight at Trev when he spoke: "You'll see us around, Buchman, unless you want to run back an' hide behind Ivy Buchman's skirts."

"Reckon you'll see me," Trev said.

He stood there at the bar and watched the Box B men file out, and then he said to Rhoda Greene, "That didn't do any good."

"You're a fool if you face them," Rhoda retorted.

"A dead fool," Ben Walters growled. He turned to McTigue, and he said sourly, "How in hell are you in this, McTigue?"

"Passin' by." McTigue smiled.

"You realize," the sheriff snapped, "that with your gun in sight this might become a full-fledged war? They wouldn't gang up on Trev alone, but now they think he's not alone."

"He's not alone." McTigue chuckled.

Ben Walters looked at Trev, and Trev said quietly, "I didn't make any deals with him, Ben."

Rhoda had left one lamp on at the far end of the bar. She walked down in that direction, and Trev followed her. She was waiting for him near the cash register.

Trev said to her, "I'm obliged, but I wish you hadn't done it."

"You killed one man in this place," Rhoda told him. "It didn't look as if your luck would hold out."

"Reckon I'm still banking on it." Trev smiled.

He touched his hat to the girl and then he walked toward the door. As he passed Ben Walters, the sheriff said to him, "I'd get to hell out. They're waiting for you, Trev."

"I'll stay," Trev told him.

Charlie Brackett walked with him as he left the saloon, and Trev said to him, "Shouldn't have brought them down, Charlie."

"Girl's idea closin' the bar," Charlie explained. "Hell, you ain't fightin' that bunch alone, Trev."

Trev looked at the six Box B horses still tied outside, a deadly reminder to him that their riders were still in town and that he could now either face them or run.

He didn't see any of them on the street, but they could have been in any of the darkened doorways between the saloons, or in the alleys, waiting for him to come to them, defying him to come.

He said to Charlie, "Better move off, Charlie. You're in the line of fire."

"I'm stayin'," Charlie said grimly.

It was nearly a hundred yards from the Wyoming Belle back to the hotel, and Trev Buchman wondered whether he would live to make it. He heard a step behind him, and then McTigue said, "I'll be across the street, Buchman."

He stepped away from them before Trev could object or even discuss the point. McTigue was in the fight if it came, a lean man with a big gun, and a string of killings of which no man knew the length.

Sheriff Walters came out of the saloon and said flatly,
"You goin' back to the hotel, I'll walk with you."

Trev looked at him. "You're asking for a gunfight,
and a big one, right in the heart of this town, Sheriff."

"I'm hoping to stop one," Ben Walters growled. "You
walk on the other side of him, Charlie. Where the hell
is McTigue?"

"Crossed the street," Charlie told him.

Trev Buchman stared up the street toward the hotel,
and then he looked at the six Box B horses at the tie
rack in front of him.

"Start walkin'," Ben Walters told him.

Trev suddenly ducked under the tie rack, untied the
nearest horse, and vaulted into the saddle. He whipped
the animal around and shot north away from the hotel
as if riding out of town.

Charlie Brackett yelled after him, and Trev caught a
glimpse of Ben Walters' amazed face. This was an action
they had not expected from him, and it had caught them
by surprise.

Trev rode at a fast gallop for about two hundred yards.
As he passed the last house on the street and was in the
shadows, he slowed down and slipped from the saddle,
letting the horse run on.

He ran for the nearest house, swinging down along
the side of it to the rear. Then he slowed down, loosening
the gun in the holster, and started back in the direction of
town, walking behind the houses along the main street.

He was in a narrow back street with a few shacks, some
of them occupied by Chinese railroad workers from the
railroad some thirty miles north of Rawdon.

Trev walked on until he came to the narrow alley between the Paradise Saloon and the Larrimore Feed Store.
The alley was no more than six feet wide, and a door
from the Paradise opened onto it. Trev remembered the
alley as he remembered so many other things about Rawdon.

Moving down it carefully, he came back to the main
street and stopped back in the shadows, keeping against
the wall of the saloon. Here he could look out on the
street without being seen.

Edging out carefully, he could see Ben Walters and
Charlie Brackett still up by the Wyoming Saloon. Rhoda
Greene had come out to join them, and they were un-

doubtedly discussing his strange behavior in suddenly
skipping town after making it plain that he intended to
stay and fight it out with Box B.

Trev looked for McTigue but couldn't find the bounty
hunter. McTigue was the kind of man who could blend
with his surroundings, and Trev was positive McTigue
was close by. He hadn't been fooled before by the horse
trick, and he wouldn't be fooled now.

It was Box B Trev was interested in, however. They
could have gone into any one of half a dozen saloons
between the Wyoming Belle and the hotel. They could
even be in the Paradise with only a wall separating them.

Trev studied the doorways and the store fronts along
the opposite side of the street. He was able to look into
the Ace High Saloon, but he couldn't make out any of the
Box B riders at the bar. The five remaining horses were
still at the tie rack, however.

From a position across the alley and a little to his rear
he heard a faint rustling sound such as an animal would
make, and he whirled his gun in that direction, the hammer back.

"Only me." McTigue chuckled. "You're hearin' good
tonight, Buchman."

"What in hell do you want?" Trev asked morosely.

It was amazing that the man had found him. He'd
been positive no one had seen him enter the alley and
he hadn't heard McTigue coming down on him from the
rear, but yet he was here.

"Box B's in the Paradise," McTigue said. "Five of 'em.
One man watchin' your crowd up at the Wyomin'. He's
in the alley next to the Ace High. You stick your head
out a little more an' he'll shoot it off."

Trev looked over toward the Ace High. He could see
the dark mouth of the alley, but he couldn't make out
anyone in it.

"See you're still ridin' horses," McTigue said with a
grin, "an' jumpin' off 'em. Figured you'd be workin'
down this side of the street. Saw you come into the Paradise."

"You don't miss much," Trev told him.

"How do you want to handle this?" McTigue asked.
"Want me to flush 'em out into the open, an' you work
on 'em when they come out? I could go in this side door,

an' when they went out onto the street I could open up on 'em, an' you'd have them in a crossfire from the alley."

"You're not in this," Trev said stiffly.

He heard McTigue chuckling again, and then McTigue's gun boomed as he shot up into the night sky.

"In it now." He laughed and darted out of the alley, cutting left out of Trev's sight.

Another gun opened from the alley next to the Ace High, and the fight was on.

Chapter Seven

TREV WATCHED the Box B riders tumbling out of the Paradise Saloon at a distance of less than ten feet. Young Langham came out first, eager for the battle. They'd heard the shot coming from the gun of their sentinel in the alley, and they knew now that their quarry was still in Rawdon.

Trev edged out to the walk as the Box B men broke and ran, three of them running past the spot where he was concealed, so close that he could almost have reached out and touched one of them.

Another man sprinted across the street to take cover with the Box B man in the Ace High alley. Langham remained where he was, brazenly waiting for his man to open up with his gun. He considered that this was his fight; he'd made his challenge very plain to Trev in the Wyoming Belle.

Trev said to him gently, "This way, Langham."

The blond gunman spun like a cat, dropping to one knee at the same time. His gun spat viciously three times, and at least one of the bullets would have caught Trev had he not stepped to the other side of the alley.

Langham's gun was following him when he squeezed on the trigger of his own gun, his bullet knocking the blond man out into the street, rolling him as if he'd been hit with a heavy club. His body bounced once, and he tried to get up, and he died there in the road, his face in the dust, the hat lying next to him.

The two men across the road opened up on Trev, who was firing steadily into the Ace High alley, and then a third gun banged from a point down the street, the direction McTigue had taken.

Lying flat on his face in the alley now, the lead singing over his head, Trev saw a Box B man stumble out of the Ace High alley clutching his stomach. He ran out to the edge of the walk as if he meant to vomit, bent over slowly, and then pitched forward on his face.

Trev jumped to his feet and ran for the side door of

the Paradise, breaking into it and entering a room behind the bar. A fat-faced bartender was just coming in from the bar, and he hurriedly stood aside to let Trev go past.

"Get 'em, Buchman!" he said.

Trev came out into the barroom, swinging around the corner of the bar. Men were watching him carefully, making no move, as he ran toward the door that opened on the street.

He pulled up behind the batwing doors, looking out into the street. Two Box B men were down, and there were still four in the fight—if they wished to continue the fight. One man was in the Ace High alley; the other three had split up and were probably in doorways along the street.

McTigue was somewhere down the street, too. It was his bullet which had knocked down the man in the Ace High alley. Where he was now was another problem— McTigue was a man who moved around.

The shooting had stopped suddenly and silence reigned over the town. Men remained indoors as yet, not knowing whether the fight was definitely finished.

Trev stood behind the batwing doors of the Paradise Saloon, his head just protruding above the top of the door, looking out into the street. If any of the Box B men saw him they would not recognize him unless they came up close, and the Paradise was the last place in which they would expect to find him.

Gun in hand, Trev waited, and then he heard Sheriff Ben Walters coming up the street, calling loudly, "That's it. That's it. I'll hang the next man throws any lead in this town."

Walters walked out in the open so that everyone could see him, and for one moment Trev wondered whether the Box B men would drop him in the street even though he wasn't in this fight.

"Buchman?" Walters called. "Trev Buchman?"

Trev didn't answer until he heard men running in the direction of the Wyoming Saloon. Then he stepped out on the walk, and saw four riders spurring away from the saloon. The remaining Box B men had had enough for this evening.

Ben Walters saw him on the walk and came over, and then Charlie Brackett ran down the street, yelling happily.

"You get around," Walters said peevishly. "Had to have your fight, didn't you?"

"They were going to set me up, Ben," Trev said. "You know that. I never would have gotten back to the hotel alive."

"We could have worked it out differently," the sheriff of Rawdon growled. "Where do you go from here?"

Trev looked down at the body of Langham sprawled in the road. Men were coming out of the saloons now, talking excitedly. A man was calling for the coroner.

"When somebody comes after you with a gun, Ben," Trev said, "you can't run away from it. You know that as well as I do."

Rhoda Greene came up behind Charlie Brackett, and Trev saw the relief in her eyes when she saw that he was still alive.

"Where's McTigue?" Charlie Brackett wanted to know. "He was in this fight, wasn't he, Trev?"

"He was in it." Trev scowled, remembering that it was McTigue who had deliberately forced the issue. He hadn't seen McTigue since the bounty hunter had run out of the alley after firing the shot that had drawn the Box B men out into the open.

Rhoda came over to Trev and said, "You'd be wise to ride out of this town and forget to come back."

"Not now." Trev smiled.

"You going out to Box B tomorrow?"

"I said I'd be out," Trev told her.

"They'll be waiting for you."

"I don't think Mrs. Buchman wants me shot up," Trev observed. "These men came out on their own tonight."

Ben Walters said grimly, "Been hell to pay ever since you hit this town, Trev. You'd be better off out of it."

Trev said evenly, "You forgetting, Ben, that Joe Fineran was shot down before I got here? I'm not running out of it now."

He went back to the hotel, Charlie Brackett going with him, and when they reached the porch they found McTigue sitting there, his boots up on the rail, hat down over his eyes.

"Feel better now?" Trev asked him tersely.

McTigue looked at him. "Somebody shot up?"

"I don't owe you anything for this," Trev told him.

McTigue put his boots down. "You were in that alley for a fight," he stated. "Don't blame it on me."

"I would've walked away from it if they had," Trev retorted. "Would you?"

McTigue sighed. "When a man lives by the gun he can expect to die by the gun. It's the way of life."

Two riders were swinging hard down the street, and Charlie Brackett said suddenly, "That's Ivy Buchman."

Trev turned to look, and as the two riders came into the light of the Paradise Saloon, he recognized Ivy Buchman and Lace Reynolds. The crowd was still out in front of the Paradise where Langham had fallen, and Ben Walters was there, also.

Ivy dismounted, and Trev saw her talking with Walters for a moment. Reynolds stood nearby, apparently disgruntled about something. Trev was positive she'd learned about the trouble brewing in town and had ridden in as fast as she could to prevent it. He wondered if Reynolds knew about his men coming here, or had it been an entirely voluntary act on their part.

"Comin' this way," Charlie murmured.

Ivy and Reynolds were moving down the walk now, crossing the street to the hotel. Trev waited for her on the porch, wondering what she would have to say.

She recognized him in the dim light on the porch, and she came up hurriedly.

"You all right, Trev?" she asked.

"All right." Trev nodded.

"I'd heard they were coming in here to make trouble for you," Ivy went on. "I came as fast as I could. Lace, here, didn't know anything about it, either."

"That right?" Trev murmured. He looked at the short, heavy-set Reynolds who was staring at him, unsmiling.

"Some of the boys didn't like it that you shot up Fogarty," Reynolds growled. "That's all there is to it, Buchman."

McTigue said from his chair, "Reckon they won't be likin' it that he shot up a few more of your riders, will they, Reynolds?"

Lace Reynolds stared at the bounty hunter, but made no answer.

"Will you be coming out to Box B?" Ivy asked, looking straight at Trev.

"I don't want a bullet in the back," Trev said.

"You won't get it in the back," Lace Reynolds murmured.

"He won't get it anywhere," Ivy flared. "Let's remember that."

"Reckon I'll be out." Trev smiled. "I'm obliged for your riding in, ma'am."

Ivy smiled, then turned and left with Reynolds.

McTigue said casually, "Nice havin' two women worried about you, Buchman. I'd watch that Reynolds, though."

"I watch everybody," Trev told him, "including you."

McTigue laughed at that, and he was still chuckling when Trev went up to his room for the night. Charlie Brackett went with him, determined to bunk with him until he went out to Box B.

"They came after you once," Charlie explained, "an' they might come again. This time I might get my gun into the fight. Last one was over afore I knew who was fightin' who."

"You'll live longer by staying out of fights like that," Trev told him. "Those boys are professionals."

He still didn't know why, though, and that fact annoyed him. Ivy Buchman and Lace Reynolds had the right, of course, to bring any kind of riders they wanted to Box B, but why gunslingers?

He knew why before the evening was over. A few minutes after they had entered his room, there was a knock on the door, and when Trev opened it, Neil Torrance, the lawyer, stood there, smiling, affable as usual.

"Thought I'd stop in for a little talk," Torrance said. "You occupied?"

"Come in," Trev said.

Torrance looked at Charlie Brackett, sitting near the window smoking a cigarette.

"This is confidential," he hinted.

Trev said over his shoulder, "Go down and buy yourself a drink, Charlie."

Charlie went out, grumbling a little, and Trev closed the door behind him. Neil Torrance had placed his brown Stetson on the table near the bed, and he sat down on the chair Charlie had just vacated. Before speaking he handed Trev a cigar. Trev nodded his thanks, putting the cigar in his vest pocket for future smoking.

"Little excitement in town tonight," Neil Torrance smiled. "You're acquiring quite a reputation with a six-gun, Buchman."

"Nothing I asked for," Trev told him quietly. "What is it you want, Torrance?"

Neil Torrance stared at him steadily. "What is it you want out at Box B?"

Trev leaned against the wall near the door. "You want that cigar back?" he asked.

The lawyer smiled. "No offense. You may need a friend around here, and I could be that friend."

"I'm not asking for friends," Trev told him.

"Still," Torrance persisted, "you are Jim Buchman's brother, and your brother's wife owns Box B, which will very shortly be the largest spread in this part of the country."

Trev looked at him. "How do you make that out?" he asked.

"Didn't your father graze all of Cannon Basin one time?" Torrance asked him.

"He was the first white man in these parts with cattle," Trev nodded.

"All range rights to Cannon Basin legally belong to him," Torrance pointed out. "I've checked that point."

"Other ranchers were coming in," Trev said, "even before he died, and my brother lost at least half of the basin after he took control of Box B."

"Ivy Buchman is going to get it back," Neil Torrance said. "All of it."

"She'll have a hell of a fight on her hands," Trev observed. "Some of these ranchers have been here for years."

"They'll get out," Neil assured him, "when Lace Reynolds and his toughs ride up to them, and Ben Walters can't do a thing about it. It'll be legal. I have definite proof that your father grazed all of the Cannon Basin."

Trev crossed the room to sit down on the edge of the bed. That was the reason, then, for the gunslingers. Ivy Buchman was getting ready to spread her wings.

"When is this going to start?" Trev asked, and then a cold chill swept over him. Had it already started? "That the reason Fogarty shot up the nester on Squaw Creek?" he asked flatly.

Torrance shrugged. "I don't know any details. I'm

handling the legal side of it. These ranchers are to be asked to vacate. If they don't they're being pushed off physically, and if they take recourse to law, they have to face me."

"You got all the ends tied up," Trev grated, still thinking of Fineran. Possibly, Joe had been used as an example. The old nester meant nothing to anybody, and possibly he'd protested when Fogarty told him he had to move out. He'd been put out of the way, and now all the ranchers and squatters in the basin knew that Ivy Buchman meant business. It was as simple as that.

"The plan is air tight," Torrance stated.

"Why tell me about it?" Trev snapped.

Even Charlie Brackett knew nothing about this move at Box B, and Charlie had been working there for more than a dozen years.

"I was under the impression," Torrance said softly, "that as Jim Buchman's brother you might be wanting something at Box B. It was too bad the estate fell into other hands."

Trev looked at him. "You'd like to make a deal with me," he said softly. "That it?"

Torrance shrugged. "Let us say that any change in the present setup would not meet with my disapproval."

"You want me to go there and put a bullet in her back?" Trev asked. "Because I might be next in line for Box B?"

Torrance smiled. "I'm here only to see how you feel," he said, "now that you know the setup."

"It's a rotten deal," Trev told him. "These other ranchers have been in Cannon Basin for years."

"Illegally," the lawyer pointed out, "and they can be moved."

"What happens to you," Trev asked him, "if I tell Mrs. Buchman that you were here talking to me."

"You won't," the lawyer told him smoothly.

"Why not?"

"Because you don't have that much love for Ivy Buchman," Torrance murmured, "remembering the odd circumstances surrounding your brother's death."

"He fell off a corral fence," Trev said.

"Of course." Neil Torrance nodded, and the derisive laughter was deep down in his brown eyes. "He had dizzy spells. Wasn't that it?"

Trev looked at the man, recognizing him for what he was. Despite his looks and impressive bearing, Neil Torrance was a little man, ready to switch his allegiance at the ring of a dollar. He knew something which Trev Buchman had to know before he could leave Cannon Basin. Trev realized that if he were to leave before he learned what that was, he would not sleep well the remainder of his life.

Chapter Eight

Ivy Buchman was waiting for him when Trev rode in to Box B the next morning with Charlie Brackett. She called him into the office where Lace Reynolds was waiting, and she said, "Lace has had a little talk with the men who made trouble for you last night, Trev. It won't happen again."

"Reckon I wouldn't like it to happen again," Trev said, looking straight at Reynolds.

Deftly, Ivy changed the subject. "Lace will talk to you about your duties," she said. "Any time you wish to see me, you'll find me around."

Trev just looked at her and nodded. He wondered what she meant by that statement. She was smiling at him warmly as she said it, and he was beginning to realize now that if he so desired he might become headman at Box B by the simple expedient of marrying Ivy Buchman. If he did so, however, he would have to be very careful when he sat on corral fences!

When Ivy went out, Lace Reynolds said sourly, "My advice to you, Buchman, is to stay the hell away from that bunkhouse down by the big corral."

"Why?" Trev smiled.

"You damn near found out why last night," Reynolds observed.

"I noticed you weren't with them," Trev told him, and he saw the red come to Reynolds' broad face. His eyes, a peculiar shade of blue, seemed to turn gray.

He said softly, "I don't know what the hell your game is here, Buchman, but you'd better walk easy."

"You're supposed to tell me my duties, not give me advice."

"All right," Reynolds snapped. "Get to hell up to White Creek with a few of the men and start that fence up along the north border of the creek."

Trev thought for a moment. "Man by the name of

Caldwell has a spread south of the Creek. You'd be fencing him in."

Lace Reynolds stared at him coldly. "Caldwell pulled out," he said simply. "You just get that fence up."

"When did he pull out?" Trev wanted to know. He remembered Tom Caldwell very well. He'd been in the basin when Bull Buchman still ran Box B, and Caldwell had been one of the few Bull had not bothered.

"You have a hell of a lot of questions," Reynolds grated. "Anything you don't like around here, you go in and see Mrs. Buchman."

"Reckon I'll ride up." Trev knew now that the drive was on. Caldwell had been pushed out, no doubt having learned what had happened to Joe Fineran at the other end of the basin. The others would be going one by one, leaving peaceably, or at the point of a gunslinger's gun. The new owner of Box B was taking over Cannon Basin.

Rounding up Charlie Brackett and two other Box B riders, Trev prepared to set out north toward White Creek. A load of fence posts and barbed wire had already been sent up to the creek, along with the necessary digging tools.

"Where we goin'?" Charlie asked when Trev told him to saddle up.

"Putting up barbed wire north of White Creek," Trev said.

Charlie had been pulling his saddle from the peg in the stable. "North?" he asked. "Hell, Trev, we'd be fencin' in Tom Caldwell."

"Caldwell's gone," Trev told him. "Box B has taken over his range."

Charlie just stared at him. "Pushed out?" he asked.

"What do you think?" Trev countered.

"Your father let Caldwell stay," Charlie muttered.

"He let Joe Fineran stay, too," Trev told him.

Charlie Brackett's blue eyes narrowed. "What in hell's goin' on around here, Trev?" he asked.

"We'll ride up to White Creek and see," Trev told him. "Saddle up."

The four of them left the ranch, following the course of the Cannon River north in the direction of White Creek. It was almost an hour's ride to the north boundary of the basin, the foothills of the Catamounts beginning on the other side of White Creek.

"Heard Reynolds wanted to string some wire up this way," Charlie Brackett said grimly. "Didn't figure he was cuttin' out Tom Caldwell, though."

"Who took up the fence posts and the wire?" Trev wanted to know.

"Lumberman in town," Charlie told him. "Saw three wagonloads goin' up that way yesterday."

As they drew near Tom Caldwell's spread, they saw smoke curling up from the chimney of the small, log ranch house, and Charlie Brackett said, "Reckon somebody's still there, Trev."

"Reynolds said he pulled out," Trev murmured. "We'll ride up."

They crossed a meadow, and then swung around a hayfield Caldwell had planted. They were within fifty yards of the log house when the rifle cracked. The bullet sang over their heads, and the four riders pulled up.

"What in hell is this?" Charlie muttered.

Trev realized that the shot had been meant only as a warning. He pulled up the gray and called sharply, "That you, Caldwell?"

"Turn around an' head back," Caldwell snapped from the house. "I have my two sons here an' my nephew. We ain't leavin' now, mister."

"Reckon he come back," Charlie Brackett said. Then he called loudly, "Tom, this is Charlie Brackett. You hear me?"

"What in hell you want?"

"Trev Buchman's with me," Charlie said. "We ain't lookin' for no trouble, Tom."

A man came out of the house, a rifle in his hands, and Trev remembered him as Tom Caldwell, a lean, thin-faced man with a long neck. He was wearing worn blue Levis and a checked shirt, and the hat on his head had a broken rim.

"Come up slow," Caldwell said suspiciously.

Trev rode up in advance of the other three Box B men. He saw two young men come out of the house and he remembered the Caldwell boys, Bob and Ames. They'd been quite young when Trev had ridden away; they were in their early twenties now.

"Both of 'em married," Charlie Brackett murmured, "an' livin' up in Ransom County. Jud, the nephew, comes from that way, too. Reckon old Tom's got himself some help."

Tom Caldwell was saying, "Heard you was back, Trev. You ridin' for Box B?"

"Signed up," Trev nodded. "What's the deal here, Tom?"

"Lace Reynolds come up here two days ago," Caldwell explained, "an' told me to get to hell off this land, that Box B was takin' it back. Had four of his toughs with him, an' one of 'em give me this eye."

Trev noticed, then, that the older man's right eye was still bruised and discolored.

"You in with this bunch?" Caldwell asked grimly. "They shot the hell outa poor Joe Fineran down by Squaw Creek."

Charlie Brackett said, "Trev, here, shot the hell outa the hombre gave it to Joe. You didn't know that, Tom?"

Tom Caldwell looked at Trev curiously. "News to me," he said. "Been hell to pay around here, Trev, since Jim died. Reckon that Reynolds an' Mrs. Buchman figure they own the whole damn earth."

"They'll try to prove they have legal right to Cannon Basin," Trev told him. "My father grazed the whole basin once, and their lawyer can prove that."

Caldwell looked at him, and then at his two sons standing just outside the doorway. "I ain't leavin'," he said. "Been runnin' stock on this land over twenty years now. Your father never bothered me way up here, Trev."

"I know." Trev nodded. "It's a new deal now."

"You in it?"

Trev smiled faintly. "No," he said.

"You're ridin' for Box B."

"Maybe I'm on your side," Trev told him. "Can you trust me, Tom?"

Tom Caldwell looked at him, and then spat. "Always could trust a Buchman," he said. "What is it you want, Trev?"

"Head back to your sons' place," Trev told him, "and stay there. You try to fight Reynolds and his crew and you'll end up like Joe Fineran."

Ames Caldwell, a big, strapping young fellow, the older

son, said quietly, "Reckon we'll take some of 'em with us, Buchman."

"They can always bring in more," Trev stated.

"What about that fence Reynolds wants to put up?" Tom Caldwell asked him. "He's got the posts an' the wire down at Coleman's Ford on the creek."

"We're supposed to put up the fence." Trev smiled. "Reckon you can let us worry about it, Tom."

Tom Caldwell shrugged. His son, Bob, said flatly, "Reckon I don't like it."

"You'll be dead you stay here," Trev warned him. "Box B has professional gunslingers on the payroll."

"We'll go." Tom Caldwell scowled. "If you can straighten this thing out with Ivy Buchman it'll be better than us throwin' lead at somebody."

The four Box B men sat on their horses watching as the Caldwell tribe saddled up and rode off, crossing the Creek and heading north toward the defile in the Catamounts.

Charlie Brackett said curiously, "What now, Trev?"

"We'll have a look at those fence posts," Trev said.

They found three wagonloads of posts and wire parked in a grove a quarter of a mile down the creek at a spot known as Coleman's Ford. The wagons were on the other side of the creek. Nearby, the horses which had pulled the wagons to the spot were grazing, taken out of harness, and waiting for the wagons to be used again.

Charlie Brackett said, "Reckon the boys brought this stuff out went back to Rawdon. We need the wagons to haul them posts as we go down the line."

Trev said, looking at the two Box B riders with them, "You trust these boys, Charlie?"

"Rode for your father." Charlie nodded. "They ain't got no use for Reynolds."

Trev shook his rope loose. "We'll leave the posts here," he said. "It's the wire we want. Have the boys push those rolls to the ground."

Charlie scratched his chin curiously, but then he helped the two Box B men roll the heavy rolls of wire off one of the wagons, bouncing them to the ground.

Trev then moved up with his rope and threw it over the nearest roll. He walked the gray down toward the fording place, dragging the roll with him and into the water. At the fording place the water was not more than

a foot deep, and Trev crossed the gray to the opposite
bank and then dragged the roll downstream into deeper
water where it was submerged.

On the bank Charlie Brackett and the two Box B riders
grinned appreciatively as Trev rode out to work his rope
loose. They then went to work on the remaining dozen
or so rolls of wire and in a matter of minutes had sunk
all of them below the surface of the creek.

Trev had them ride their horses back and forth for another half-hour, obliterating the drag marks in the ground.
Then they turned and rode south back toward Box B.

"Can't string up no damned wire," Charlie grinned,
"when there ain't any wire. That right, boys?"

Back at Box B Trev found Lace Reynolds down at one
of the corrals where some yearlings were being branded.
Reynolds looked at him suspiciously as he rode up.

It was only a little past high noon, and they were supposed to have spent the day setting up the wire on the
other side of the creek.

"You're back early," Reynolds said grimly.

"Can't string wire without the wire," Trev observed.
"You forget to send it out?"

Lace Reynolds looked at him. "I went out with those
wagons, myself, yesterday," he grated. "The rolls were
on the wagon."

"Plenty of posts," Trev told him. "No wire."

"You're a damned liar," Reynolds said softly.

Trev looked at him for a moment, and then dismounted
to tie his gray to a corral post.

"Wire's gone," he said.

"The wire was on those wagons up at White Creek,"
Lace Reynolds snarled. "There's nobody in this part of
the country has the guts to take it off, except you."

Trev smiled at him. "Reckon I'll talk to Mrs. Buchman
about it," he said, and he turned away.

"You'll talk to me," Reynolds raged, and grasping him
by the arm, spun him around.

Trev said softly, "Don't touch me again, Reynolds."

"You'll talk to me," the Box B ramrod snarled.

"Take off that gunbelt," Trev invited.

Several Box B men were standing nearby, grinning, and
then several more came down from the direction of the
bunkhouse, anticipating a brawl.

"I'll take it off," Reynolds said slowly, "but you'll wish to hell I hadn't, mister."

Both men unbuckled their gunbelts, and then Trev waited for his man to come in. He realized that he was against a tough man with incredible strength. Reynolds was built like a bull—close to the ground, tremendous shoulders, a short, thick neck. He was inches shorter than Trev, but considerably the heavier man, and he would use that weight this afternoon.

Reynolds rushed, swinging both short, ponderous arms, aiming for Trev's body. This would be the pattern of the fight—he would try to wear Trev down with those solid smashes to the body and then cut and rip him to pieces when his guard came down.

Trev moved away, chopping at Reynolds' head as he lumbered past him, and drawing blood with the first punch. The left cheekbone was cut, and blood started to trickle down Reynolds' face.

"Easy does it," Charlie Brackett called. "Don't let him wear you out, Trev."

Reynolds righted himself and came in again, his thick fists whipping through the air, one of them nearly catching Trev in the ribs. Again Trev lashed at the short man's face, catching him squarely in the right eye this time.

Reynolds blinked and staggered back, pawing at the eye with one of his hands. It started to swell up immediately, and in a matter of moments he could scarcely see out of it.

Trev circled his man, avoiding those lunges, keeping away from the corral fence, knowing that once Reynolds got him against a wall he would be finished.

He had longer arms, and he was built strongly, himself, and whenever Reynolds missed him, he whipped at him with both fists, drawing blood from Reynolds' nose, and then from his smashed lips.

The Box B ramrod fought silently, oblivious to the punishment he was absorbing, and Trev realized that he could go on this way all afternoon. But sooner or later he would close with his man.

"Stay away from him," Charlie warned as Reynolds rushed again, peering at Trev out of one good eye.

As Trev smashed him again with his right fist, and then

his left, aiming now for Reynolds' good eye, he caught a glimpse of Ivy Buchman hurrying down from the house. He wondered if she would try to stop it.

There wasn't any time to watch her, though, because Reynolds was constantly boring in at him, and once he did catch Trev in the right side, and the blow was sufficient to knock Trev off his feet.

He rolled, though, when Lace Reynolds drove in at him, and he was up on his feet again before Reynolds could pin him to the ground. His right side felt numb, and a lot of the wind had been taken out of him.

Reynolds tore in triumphantly, and then Trev lashed out hard with his right fist, and this time he landed on the target. Reynolds staggered, and his left eye dripped blood from the cut underneath it and started to swell as had the other eye.

It would be only a matter of time now before Reynolds would be partially and temporarily blinded, but the Box B man still came at him, terrific power in his short, powerful arms.

Trev stayed away from him. He didn't like to do it, but he had no choice now—it was a case of himself or Reynolds. He continued to slash at Lace Reynolds' eyes, cutting them to ribbons until Reynolds' face was a horrible mask at which he pawed with both hands, trying to clear the blood from his eyes so that he could see and continue the fight.

Now and then he caught Trev glancing blows in the ribs, and a second time he floored his man, but again was unable to follow up his advantage. Trev scrambled up and continued to slash at him. Once he backed Reynolds against the corral and hit him hard at least eight times in succession before Reynolds, through bull strength, pushed him away.

The man's left eye was completely closed now, and he could see only dimly through the right. Trev deliberately kept away from him now, refusing even to hit him, waiting for the right eye to close.

When it did, he walked away from his man, his own hands bruised and swollen, and his ribs purple from the pounding Reynolds had given him.

Lace Reynolds moved forward, searching for him, and

then two of his riders stepped forward and held him, and then led him down to the bunkhouse, still protesting, wanting to go on with the fight.

Ivy Buchman came over to Trev and said softly, "Come into the house. I'll see what I can do for those hands."

He understood how it was with her, then. Ivy Buchman liked a winner.

Chapter Nine

THERE WERE no bones broken in Trev's hands, but the knuckles were cut and bruised and so swollen that he could scarcely hold the coffee cup Ivy handed to him. She had helped him wash his hands in warm water, and she'd cleaned the few small cuts he'd sustained on his face, and then she'd poured him a cup of coffee from the pot on the kitchen stove.

Trev said to her, "You take good care of the relatives."

Ivy smiled. She stood very close to him, looking down at him, her amber eyes glowing.

"You still haven't told me what the fight was about," she said. "I realized you two didn't exactly like each other, but I was surprised to see you go this far."

"We had a few words," Trev admitted. "Had to do with that barbed wire fence Reynolds wanted built north of White Creek."

Ivy looked at him. "What about it?" she asked.

"You pushed Tom Caldwell off his land," Trev said.

"My land." Ivy smiled. "Cannon Basin belongs to Box B. All of it."

Trev shook his head. "When a man has grazed his stock on a piece of range for over twenty years, you just can't tell him to move off."

"Wouldn't you like to see Box B back to where it was?" Ivy asked. "As big as it was when your father settled here?"

Trev looked at her. "That's your ambition?" he asked.

"Is it bad, Trev?" she wanted to know. "Legally, Cannon Basin belongs to Box B. I am only claiming that which I own."

"You'll have a range war on your hands," Trev warned her. "These ranchers aren't going to pull out just because you say so."

"Neil Torrance says they can be evicted by processes of law, if necessary," Ivy informed him.

Trev was thinking that Neil Torrance was ready to double-cross her the moment he saw the opportunity to advance himself. He had said as much in the hotel room the other night.

"You have a lot of ambition," Trev murmured. "If you get control of the entire Cannon Basin, you'll be the biggest rancher in this part of the country."

"That would be good, wouldn't it?" Ivy asked him softly. "I wouldn't be forgetting, of course, that you are a very close relative."

I could be closer, too, Trev thought, if I want to forget about Jim, and about men like Fineran and Tom Caldwell.

"Now tell me exactly what the quarrel was about?" Ivy said. "What about the fence up at White Creek?"

"Reynolds sent some posts and barbed wire up to the creek," Trev stated. "Reynolds didn't like it that the wire disappeared."

"Disappeared?"

Trev nodded blandly.

"Where did you put it?" she asked him, a grin breaking out on her face.

Trev studied her for a moment. "Under White Creek," he said. "You can fish it out whenever you want to."

She laughed aloud, then, and Trev lifted his coffee cup to his lips. When he put it down, Ivy Buchman came over and kissed him squarely on the mouth. She said softly, "I liked that, your hiding the wire on Reynolds."

"You going to put up that fence?" Trev asked her. He could still feel her lips upon his. She was a highly attractive woman, and she wanted him in on this deal.

"Eventually," Ivy said, "I'm going to put up the fence. I intend to fence in the entire basin some day."

"You'll have it running with blood," Trev warned her. "You'll need a regiment of gunthrowers to keep it for you."

"I'll get them if I have to," Ivy Buchman told him calmly. "I intend to keep that which belongs to me."

"It's yours to do with as you wish," Trev said quietly, "but don't count me in on it."

"You're quitting?"

"Right now. You want men like Reynolds and Fogarty for this kind of work."

"I didn't sign you up to use a gun or a club," Ivy snapped. "You're here to work the stock."

"Sooner or later," Trev told her, "it will come to that.

I have friends in Cannon Basin. Reckon I don't like to see them hurt."

He picked up his hat from the table, and then he turned toward the door, and he saw the disappointment in Ivy Buchman's eyes. She stood there, frowning at him, her beautiful lips tight, and then she said, "You're a fool, Trev."

"What is the word for you?" Trev asked her softly, and he left her with that.

He realized that he'd made a bitter enemy. Ivy Buchman had cast herself at him, and he'd turned her down. She would never forget that as long as they both lived.

Outside, Trev met Charlie Brackett. "Reckon she's on your side, Trev."

"No more," Trev told him. "I'm through at Box B."

Charlie frowned at him. "Quit?" he asked. When Trev nodded, he said, "Reckon that's enough for me, too, Trev. Ride in with you."

"This is your job," Trev argued.

"Not any more," Charlie said grimly. "I don't take orders from Lace Reynolds."

Ivy was standing on the porch watching them a few minutes later as Trev and Charlie came out of the bunkhouse with their saddlebags.

"Reckon she don't look happy." Charlie grinned. "You cross her, Trev?"

"I crossed her."

"An' what happens now?" Charlie asked curiously. "You leavin' this part of the country?"

"Figured I'd stay around a while," Trev told him. He wasn't sure, himself, just why, except that he knew he couldn't leave. In one sense he'd assured the Caldwells that he'd be on their side, and he couldn't back down on that promise now. It wasn't clear as yet how he could help them, but he had to remain in the area.

Back in Rawdon they found McTigue waiting on the porch of the hotel as they came up. The bounty hunter did not seem surprised to see them. "Reckon you didn't last long, Buchman. Have it out with Reynolds?"

Trev fingered one of the small cuts on his face which had made it obvious to McTigue that he'd been in a fight.

"I had it out," Trev said.

"Find out what you wanted to know?"

Trev looked down at the lean man with the sharp nose. "What do I want to know?" he countered.

"I asked you." McTigue grinned.

Trev had no more to say to him. He registered at the hotel, getting his old room back. Then he had supper with Charlie Brackett, and after supper headed down toward the Wyoming Belle.

Rhoda Greene was waiting for him when he came in, apparently having heard that he was back in town. She came over immediately as Trev stood at the bar with Charlie Brackett, and she said, "I understand you've made some more enemies."

"Easy to make an enemy." Trev smiled.

"Reynolds will never stop now till he sees you dead," Rhoda said quietly. "I heard about the fight."

"You want me to run?" Trev asked.

"You saw what happened after you shot Fogarty," Rhoda warned him. "What do you think will happen now?"

Trev shrugged. "We'll watch it," he said.

"You know what the talk is in this town now?"

"What?" Trev asked curiously.

"There are more than a dozen ranchers in the Cannon Basin who will be squeezed out," Rhoda told him, "if Ivy Buchman has her way. Those men are banding together against Reynolds' gunthrowers, and they're looking to you for leadership. You're the man shot down two of the Box B crew, and now you've whipped Reynolds himself. What are you going to do?"

Trev frowned at this. "They want to fight Box B?" he asked. "Ivy has the law on her side, according to Neil Torrance. She can prove my father grazed all of the basin, and has legal right to it."

"She can only enforce that right with guns," Rhoda pointed out. "Some of these ranchers have been on the land a long time. They'll claim squatters' rights, if nothing else. I doubt if Ben Walters will help Mrs. Buchman drive these ranchers away."

Trev didn't think Walters would, either. The sheriff of Rawdon would try to maintain a hands-off policy as much as he could, but when the shooting began he would have to be in it.

Charlie Brackett, who had been listening in, scratched

his jaw and said, "What do you figure to gain by this, Trev? You help the ranchers keep their land, an' you get a bullet in the back from one of Reynolds' riders."

"They want to pay you for this." Rhoda Greene smiled. "That's the talk I hear."

"Pay me!" Trev stared.

"It's like a cattlemen's association, with all ranchers in it except Box B," Rhoda explained. "There'll be a fee for you to throw your gun on their side."

"Against your own land," Charlie muttered.

"It's not his land any more," Rhoda said. "Here's Wes Hampton of Anchor Ranch. I think he wants to talk with you, Trev."

The girl moved away, tall, head erect, and men followed her with their eyes as she walked.

Wes Hampton, whom Trev had known in the old days, came up to the bar, two other men with him, whom Trev did not know. Hampton was a man in his fifties, an established rancher with a family now. He'd been in the basin at least fifteen years, and Trev could see that he wasn't going to leave without a fight.

Hampton had round shoulders, and he was clumsily built—his arms were too short, he was too heavy in the stomach—but Trev remembered him as a hard worker who'd started on a shoestring and had built up his Anchor Ranch to the point where it was second largest in the basin.

"Hear you had a little trouble over at Box B today," Wes began.

"Everybody knows my business," Trev murmured.

Wes came right to the point. "Rhoda been telling you about our plans?" he asked.

Trev nodded.

"We're lining up all the ranchers in the basin," Hampton told him. "We still have to get men like Tom Caldwell and one or two others up near White Creek. We want you in on it, Trev."

"You want my gun," Trev corrected him.

"For a hundred and fifty a month," Hampton said quietly. "It looks to us as if you're lined up against Box B already. You'll be getting paid now to work in with us."

"Think you can beat Mrs. Buchman?" Trev asked him.

"Not without you," Hampton stated. "We know what

you can do around here now, Trev. We'd like you on
our side. We're paying the salary because you don't stand
to make anything on this if we win. All of us figure you
got a pretty bad break."

Trev said, "I'd be a damned fool, Hampton, to buck
Box B unless I had a pretty good reason to do it."

"None of us know why you came back," Hampton
pointed out. "If you got reasons for coming here, and
reasons for staying, you might just as well take our money
and work in with us."

Trev could see now the way this town was thinking.
Every man in Rawdon assumed he'd come back to Cannon Basin to regain possession of Box B. He'd been fighting Ivy Buchman's crew ever since he got here, and they
thought he would continue to do so, especially if he were
offered a salary.

"You stay here," Hampton urged, "and you're in the
fight anyway. This way you have us with you."

"I don't sell my gun," Trev said, and he saw the disappointment come into the man's faded blue eyes. "I'll use
it," he finished, "when I think I must."

Hampton brightened. "Then you figure on staying in
Rawdon?"

"When I'm ready to ride," Trev said, "I'll ride. I'm not
ready, yet."

Hampton and his friends had to be satisfied with that.
They left him just as Sheriff Ben Walters came in. Walters
picked his way through the tables to the bar where Trev
was standing. He said glumly, "Been hell to pay since
you hit this town, Trev. Reckon you know about Hampton
and the others lining up against Box B?"

"I know about it," Trev nodded.

"So now you've killed off three Box B riders, and you've
whipped Reynolds, and that puts you on Hampton's
side."

Trev smiled. "I'm on my own side, Ben," he stated.
"Reckon that's the way I want it."

"You didn't throw in with Hampton?"

"No," Trev shook his head.

"Anybody needs friends in this town," Walters said
gruffly, "you do, but it's your business. I'm riding over
to Box B tomorrow to talk to Ivy Buchman. Maybe I can
get her to forget this crazy scheme."

"You won't," Trev told him, "and it's not a crazy

scheme. She gets away with it she stands to own the richest range land in the state—water, grass, winter range, everything."

"She's gambling high," Walters admitted. "I don't know if she can make this thing stick in a court of law. Some of these boys have been grazing Cannon Basin for a long time."

Trev looked down at the bar. He said, "Ivy will be bringing in more gunhands when she hears the ranchers in the basin are uniting. There'll be hell to pay." He had another thought, then, and he said, "You know who McTigue is after?"

Ben Walters wrinkled his big nose in disgust. "I don't go for his kind," he said. "A peace officer is one thing; a bounty hunter after blood money is another. McTigue's kind don't tell anybody anything."

After Ben Walters left, Trev stood at the bar for some time with Charlie Brackett. He was aware of the fact that men were watching him, discussing him, and probably wondering what his course of action would be. He was the question mark in this town. If he went with the ranchers opposed to Box B, he would undoubtedly draw others in with him, and their fight against Ivy Buchman could be successful. Without him, they were hesitant. A movement like this needed a leader, a man who carried a big gun, and knew how to use it.

Rhoda Greene came back to him and said, "My advice to you is to get out, Trev. You have nothing to gain here."

"I'd like to know what happened to Jim before I leave," Trev murmured.

Rhoda stared at him. "You've come around to that," she said slowly.

"You knew Jim as well as anybody," Trev told her. "You think he was killed?"

"I don't know," Rhoda confessed. "There were no witnesses, except Lace Reynolds. That's all I know about it."

Trev sat in at a card game with Charlie Brackett and two other men who'd known him in the old days, and when he pulled out of it, the hour was past midnight.

Charlie lingered behind to play a few more hands as Trev stepped out on the porch. A man was lounging against one of the porch pillars nearby, a cigarette glowing in his mouth. As Trev passed him, the man said, "See you're still alive."

It was McTigue.

Trev pulled up. He said sourly, "You never sleep?"

"Too much business in this town." The bounty hunter grinned. "Reckon you're in the middle of it, Buchman."

Trev stared at him. "What kind of business?" he asked.

"Box B offered fifteen hundred dollars to the man can run you out of Rawdon."

Trev laughed softly. "It's a lot of money," he said. "Who was it offered to?"

"Me." McTigue smiled.

Trev Buchman stepped back and leaned against the pillar on the other side of the porch. He said, "You taking the job?"

McTigue's grin broadened. "It's a hell of a lot of money," he admitted. "I'm thinkin' about it, Buchman."

"You'll have a hell of a time collecting it, too," Trev observed.

McTigue shrugged. "When I take a job," he said softly, "I usually collect, Buchman."

Trev left him standing there on the porch, smoking his cigarette. McTigue hadn't admitted that he was taking the job, but whether he took it or not, one thing was certain. Ivy Buchman had put a killer on his trail. Had she done the same thing to Jim in order to get the range she now was seeking to keep?

Chapter Ten

TREV WAS HAVING his breakfast the next morning in the hotel dining room when a boy brought him a note from Neil Torrance. The lawyer wanted to see him in his office, if it was convenient, that morning.

Slipping the note into his shirt pocket, Trev finished his breakfast. Walking down the street a few minutes later, he thought he knew why Torrance wanted to see him. The sides were being drawn up in Cannon Basin now, and Torrance, who had been in with Box B, was now contemplating switching his allegiance. Possibly, Ivy Buchman and Lace Reynolds were pushing him out into the cold, and it was necessary for him to start feathering his own nest.

A narrow stairway led up to Torrance's office on the second floor of the building which housed the Paradise Saloon. Trev went up the stairs, finding Torrance's door open when he reached the top.

The lawyer sat with his boots up on his desk, a cigar in his mouth, looking out through the dusty window on the main street of Rawdon.

Trev said to him, "Sure you want to see me, Torrance?"

Neil Torrance smiled. "Close the door and sit down, Buchman."

Trev closed the door behind him. He leaned against the wall instead of sitting down, and he rolled a cigarette as Neil Torrance watched him casually.

"Wouldn't be too good for you, would it," he asked, "if Reynolds saw you with me?"

"To hell with Reynolds," Torrance said.

"What's on your mind?" Trev asked him.

"You throwing in with the ranchers against Box B?" Torrance asked him.

"My business," Trev said.

Torrance grinned, revealing even white teeth. "What if I could help you get back Box B," he said. "Would that be your business or not?"

77

Trev just looked at him. "You're a lawyer," he said. "Talk sense."

"If I help you get back Box B, will you give me a third share in the outfit?"

"I don't make deals with anybody," Trev told him. "You're wasting my time, Torrance."

"It's a fair proposition," Torrance urged. "You're a damned fool to turn it down."

"I'm turning it down," Trev said and put his hand on the doorknob.

Neil Torrance said to him evenly, "Your brother was murdered, Buchman. I'm convinced he was slugged and pushed into that corral."

Trev turned around and leaned against the wall again. His face was expressionless, but paler than it had been before.

"You saw it?" he asked.

"A rider by the name of Tug Andrews saw something," Torrance told him grimly. "Andrews used to ride for Lace Reynolds. A few days after your brother was killed, Andrews dropped out of sight. I happened to run across him over in Carney three weeks ago. He needed a few drinks, and I bought the drinks for him. He made some remarks."

"Who did he name?" Trev asked softly.

"Nobody directly," Torrance stated, "but he'd seen something out at Box B, and Lace Reynolds had paid him off to keep his mouth shut and get out of this part of the country. Andrews hadn't gotten as far away as he should have."

"He still in Carney?" Trev wanted to know.

"He could be," Torrance nodded. "He was broke and riding for a man named Corwin."

Trev Buchman turned, opened the door and started down the stairs. He could hear Torrance calling after him, but he didn't stop. For the first time since coming to Rawdon he had something into which he could sink his teeth. There had been a witness besides Lace Reynolds, and Reynolds had paid off that witness and sent him packing, and that had been his mistake.

Saddling the gray gelding at the Fairfax Stables, Trev rode out of town, glad that he hadn't run across Charlie Brackett because Charlie surely would have insisted upon going along. Charlie had been having his hair cut in the barber shop adjoining the hotel, and Trev left him there.

He rode north out of Rawdon in the direction of the Catamount Mountains. Carney was a small town on the other side of the Catamounts, a town reached only by a stagecoach road. Trev remembered it as a collection of a dozen or more buildings. It may have become slightly larger now, but he doubted that.

Moving up the stage road for several miles, he turned west into Cannon Basin, taking a short cut over the hills. He had to pass Wes Hampton's place, which was near the east end of White Creek, and he noticed how Wes had improved his spread since he'd been here last.

He kept clear of the ranch, however, not wanting to run into Wes or anyone else. Tom Caldwell's ranch lay several miles to the east, and he wondered if Reynolds had come back to dredge for his barbed wire in the creek. . . .

By late afternoon Trev was moving through the Catamounts through a defile known as Mexican Pass. The town of Carney lay at the other end of the pass, still a distance of five or six miles away. This was wild country, heavily wooded in spots, and for some distance the gray gelding moved through a stand of Douglas fir, walking on brown pine needles.

Again Trev had the feeling that he was being followed —the same feeling he'd had the night he'd found Joe Fineran dying, when McTigue, the bounty hunter, had been behind him on the road.

Several times Trev stopped in the pass, listening carefully, and he fancied that he could hear the soft thud of a horse's hoofs, but when he stopped to ascertain the fact, the sound stopped also.

He wondered if McTigue were actually following him. If he were, it could mean that the bounty hunter had decided to try for that fifteen hundred dollars.

The pass already lay in the shadows as Trev pushed on toward Carney, listening carefully as he rode. On the pine needles it was difficult hearing anything, but when he had come out of the trees he could distinctly hear the thud of a horse's hoofs. It was slow and measured, keeping beat with his own, and always remaining the same distance away.

There was only one way to check on a man trailing him, and Trev wasted no time. He started ahead at a sharp trot, moved several hundred yards, and then suddenly swung the gray to the right and started a wide circle which would bring him up on the rear of his trailer.

With a man like McTigue a more obvious tactic, such as pulling off the side of the trail and waiting for his man to come up, would not work. McTigue, if it was McTigue, had ears like a cat, and he would know when his man had stopped, and he would stop, also.

Trev rode hard coming back on his trail, but at a distance of about fifty yards to the right of the trail, and then he swung back behind the rider who had been following him.

The maneuver was designed to throw his pursuer into a state of confusion, but on this occasion it did not. When Trev eventually came back upon his own trail and the trail of the man who had been coming behind him, he heard a rider galloping hard in the distance, heading for Carney.

If it were McTigue who had been behind him, the bounty hunter had easily discerned his purpose, and instead of holding up, he'd pushed his horse forward so that it was impossible now for Trev to catch up with him. Carney lay only a few more miles to the north, and the rider was hammering hard in that direction. With the shadows settling in the hills here it would also be impossible to see him.

Chagrined, Trev turned the gray north again, wondering now what he would find in Carney. He'd come after a man, and someone had come after him and would be waiting for him somewhere in the small town ahead.

It was nearly dusk when he rode out of the hills and descended to the scattered collection of faded, false-front houses along the single street which was Carney. He had been right in assuming that Carney had not grown as had Rawdon. It was possible that it had become even smaller, if anything, because less than half of the buildings were illuminated. Undoubtedly, Rawdon, having the railroad, had drawn people from Carney, and Carney was now little more than a ghost town, possibly the hangout for wanted men and loose riders.

There were a few horses tied at the tie rack of the only saloon in town. The second saloon had been closed down, and its porch was sagging. Several other buildings along the street were about ready to collapse, with the grass growing right up to the doors.

Pulling up at the saloon, Trev dismounted, and as he did so, a man came out of a building across the road and looked at him for a moment before going back in.

Moving past the three horses at the tie rack, Trev ran a hand over the flanks of each animal. There was no sweat, which meant that the man who had been ahead of him had not tied his horse here. He could have pulled up at any one of the dozen or so shacks and stables to conceal his mount.

Entering the saloon, Trev found about half a dozen customers and one bartender. All of them looked at him suspiciously as he came up to the bar. The bartender was a fat man with a dirty apron around his waist and a cigar stub in his mouth.

He worked a rag along the bar as he came down to where Trev was standing, and he said, "Ridin' through?"

Trev shook his head. "Tug Andrews around here?" he asked.

The fat man chewed on his cigar and frowned. "Law man?" he said grimly.

"Name's Buchman," Trev said. "My father was Bull Buchman, back in the basin."

The fat bartender's eyes widened. "Reckon you must be the one rode out years ago. Heard about you. What in hell you want with Andrews?"

"Talk," Trev said. "He come in here?"

"Sooner or later." The bartender nodded affably. "Ain't no other place in town for a drinkin' man, an' Tug is a drinkin' man."

"He still riding for Corwin?" Trev asked.

"Not any more. Jesse Corwin got rid of him. He ain't sober often enough to handle stock."

Trev had a drink at the bar and paid for it, and then he stood there, the glass in his hand, looking around the room. Two men stood at the other end of the bar, and the others sat at a card table. They'd all watched him when he came in, but they'd relaxed a little when they saw the bartender greet him as a friend and not as a peace officer.

Taking his drink to a corner table, Trev sat down with it. When the bartender passed him once, taking drinks to the card table, he said, "Any place a man can eat in this town?"

"My wife can fix up some steak an' eggs in the back," the fat man told him. "That good enough for you?"

"That'll do it." Trev nodded.

He sat there, nursing the drink, wondering if Tug Andrews would talk with enough pressure put upon him.

In a matter of minutes the bartender's wife had the meal ready for him, and Trev passed through a door to one side of the bar, and into the kitchen. When he sat down at the table he said to the bartender, "Tell Andrews to come in here. I'll buy him a drink."

"He'll be damned glad to hear that." The fat man grinned. "He ain't buyin' many of his own these days."

As he was going back to the bar, Trev called after him idly, "Don't tell him who it is. This is a surprise."

"For a free drink," the bartender chuckled, "Andrews would come in to see the devil himself."

Trev went at the steak and the eggs hungrily. He'd had a late breakfast that morning, and he hadn't eaten since, and he judged the time to be about seven o'clock in the evening now.

The bartender's wife had set the food on the table for him, and then left for another part of the house. The price had been four bits, and she'd seemed satisfied with that. She'd left a coffeepot on the table, and twice Trev filled his cup as he ate. He was filling it the third time when a man came in through the door from the bar.

He was a small, seedy-looking man with wisps of faded blond hair sticking out from his battered hat. He had the shiny face and the bloodshot eyes of the habitual drinker.

The bartender called in after him, "Here's Andrews, mister."

Andrews stood in front of the table, looking down at Trev. He wore a gun on his left side, and he had a cast in one eye.

"You want to see me?" he asked.

"Sit down," Trev told him. "I'll buy you a drink."

"Always can use a drink." Andrews grinned. He went outside and got the drink himself, setting it down on the table and then taking a seat across from Trev. "You know me, mister?" he asked.

"I know you," Trev nodded. "You knew my brother."

Andrews stared at him and then downed his drink.

"Jim Buchman," Trev said. "You saw him killed."

Tug Andrews pushed his chair back and wiped his mouth with the back of his sleeve. "Who in hell says that?" he demanded.

"You saw Lace Reynolds knock him off that corral fence," Trev went on evenly, "maybe with the butt of a gun. Was that what he used, Andrews?"

"You're crazy as all hell," Andrews blurted out.

"Reynolds paid you to get the hell out of this part of the country," Trev went on, "but you didn't get far enough. You're riding back with me to Rawdon to tell this story to Sheriff Walters."

He was prepared for Andrews' next move because he expected it. When Andrews went for his gun, Trev was on top of him like a cat, smashing at his wrist with the heel of his hand, grabbing Andrews, then, by the shirt front and slamming him into a chair. He hit him once with his fist, a short, jolting blow which would not have bothered another man too much, but was sufficient to knock Andrews into a state of semiconsciousness.

As he sagged in the chair, Trev lifted his gun from the holster, and then walked over to an open window to drop it out. He waited until Andrews recovered and then said to him, "You want to ride back to Rawdon peaceably, or must I tie you to the saddle?"

Andrews glared at him. "You know what in hell Reynolds will do to me, don't you?"

"We'll give you protection," Trev promised him, "until you testify."

"Protection!" Andrews sneered. "Reynolds an' his crew will shoot the hell out of you boys, an' then he'll fill me full of lead."

"Where's your horse?" Trev asked him. "You tied out front?"

"Find him yourself," Andrews growled.

Trev lifted his gun from the holster. "We'll go out that rear door—" he nodded toward a door which apparently opened on a rear yard behind the saloon. "You make a break and you'll be dead without ever having to see Reynolds or anyone else."

Andrews just stared up at him from the chair, and then Trev stepped forward and yanked him to his feet, shoving him toward the door. They went out into the night together, Trev a step or two behind his man, and they walked around to the front of the saloon where the horses were tied. A sorrel horse was tied next to his own at the tie rack, along with the other three horses which had been there before.

"Get up in the saddle," Trev ordered.

Andrews was about to obey when they heard horsemen coming in from the south, moving fast up the stage road. Rapidly, Trev untied the gray gelding and led the horse around the corner of the building, pushing Tug Andrews ahead of him.

A few moments later five riders drew up in front of the saloon, and in the dim light from inside Trev recognized Lace Reynolds as one of them. Reynolds' face was criss-crossed with pieces of adhesive tape from the cuts he'd sustained in the fight.

As Reynolds started to dismount, Andrews, who was in front of Trev, but concealed in the shadows at the corner of the building, yelled suddenly, "Reynolds! Buchman's over here."

He broke away from Trev, then, running out into the open, heading for Lace Reynolds, who stood on the other side of his horse.

Trev held his gun on the running man, knowing that he could not shoot him. To stop Andrews he would have to put a bullet in the man's back. Andrews seemed to have sensed that he wouldn't do this.

As Andrews came out into a patch of lamplight from the saloon, Lace Reynolds' gun spoke twice. He shot across the saddle, resting his gun on the seat of the saddle, and Trev saw Andrews suddenly go down as if he'd been tripped.

His body hit the ground and his hat rolled from his head, and then he tried to get up on hands and knees and pull himself forward toward the man who had shot him, but Reynolds put a third bullet into him at a distance of less than fifteen feet. Andrews collapsed on the ground, then, and lay there in the lamplight, both hands twitching as he died.

"Get him," Reynolds snapped at his men.

Two of them were still in the saddle. They swerved their horses out away from the tie rack, swinging out into the darkness, and then coming around at Trev so that the corner of the building was no protection.

Trev fired carefully at one of the riders, saw him sag in the saddle, and then turned his attention to Reynolds, who had run up on the saloon porch. Reynolds was already out of the line of fire, ordering his men to get around to the rear of the building to cut Trev off that way.

It was then that a gun started to bark from a building directly across from the saloon. One of the two men who'd come after Trev on horseback fell from the saddle, and then lead started to smash into the building at about the place where Lace Reynolds had taken refuge.

"Knock him down," Reynolds boomed. "Knock that one down."

It was time for Trev to go. With the new gun still banging, he made a dash for the gray which was standing a dozen feet away. Vaulting into the saddle, he shot away from the building and out into the road.

"Drop him!" Reynolds roared.

Lead flew after Trev as he hammered down the road for about a hundred yards. Then he slowed the gray down and slipped from the saddle, letting the horse run on as he cut for the nearest building.

There was a fight still going on in this town, and the man who had enabled him to get clear was still there. Reynolds' gunhands would begin to close in on him now that Trev himself was gone.

Trev headed back toward the building from which the shots had been fired. As he ran he kept back in the shadows, and then he swung around behind what looked to be an abandoned stable and saw a man running toward him.

He didn't think Reynolds' men had time as yet to get to the rear of the building where the gunman had been concealed, which could only mean that Trev's rescuer was coming up toward him.

"This way," Trev called sharply.

The runner cut in toward him as he stood in the shadows of the old barn, and when he was up close, breathing hard, Trev heard the old familiar chuckle of McTigue, the bounty hunter.

"Close enough." McTigue grinned. "You get in the damnedest scrapes, Buchman."

"Whose side you on now?" Trev growled. "You forget about that fifteen hundred?"

"Might pick it up later." McTigue laughed. "Reckon we'd better be off now. They're comin' up."

They could hear men moving through the night, coming on foot up the street. Then they heard Lace Reynolds' heavy voice: "One of them didn't get out. Only one horse moved out of this town."

"Your horse trick worked this time," McTigue whispered.

"Where's your horse?" Trev asked him.

"Shack farther up," McTigue said. "No damned use runnin'. There's only four of 'em now, an' they think one of us."

"You follow me out of Rawdon?" Trev asked him.

"Saw you ridin'," McTigue said. "I was out in the hills. You were bein' watched, an' I figured Reynolds would be sendin' some of his boys after you. I tagged along. Reckon I was right about Reynolds." He paused, and then he said, "Who was the hombre Reynolds shot down?"

Trev hesitated before answering, and then he remembered that McTigue had gone out on a limb for him tonight and was now endangering his life by being here.

"He went by the name of Andrews," Trev explained. "Seems he saw Lace Reynolds kill my brother."

McTigue whistled softly. "How in hell did Reynolds miss him the first time?" he asked.

"Paid him off," Trev said, "but Andrews didn't go far enough."

There was no more time to talk now because they could hear Reynolds saying, "We'll search every damned building in the town. This one's not getting away."

They could hear two riders moving up fast toward the other end of the town to prevent anyone moving out from that end. Reynolds himself seemed to be moving directly toward the shack behind which they were hiding.

Chapter Eleven

McTigue said softly, "Time to move. Follow me, Buchman."

Trev followed him, realizing that McTigue had an uncanny way of extricating himself from trouble. They moved up past several houses, one of which was occupied. A dog came growling at them, and McTigue called to the dog softly, and when the dog approached, wagging his tail, Trev saw McTigue's right hand rise and fall, and the dog lay on the ground.

"Don't like to pistol-whip a dog," he said to Trev, "but this one could have cost us our lives."

They could hear the two riders coming down the street again, riding slowly, watching for any movement between the buildings, and again they crouched against a wall at the back of a house and waited.

Down the street they could hear Reynolds talking with a man who had come out to see what they wanted.

"In here," McTigue said, and Trev followed him into a shed where he could make out the faint outlines of a horse.

McTigue led the horse out into the open, holding its nose so that the animal wouldn't snort or whinny. Out in the street they could see the two Box B riders going down the street slowly toward where Reynolds was standing.

"What now?" Trev whispered.

"Had your horse," McTigue said, "we could just make a break for it, an' to hell with 'em. Ride double an' they'll shoot us both out of the saddle."

"You move out," Trev advised. "You should be able to get clear of them with this roan, and they'll think we're both gone, then."

McTigue shook his head. "They'll pick up your gelding up the road," he said, "an' they'll come gunnin' back for you. If Reynolds thinks you got something on him you'll never leave this town alive."

A rider was coming down the alley between two buildings and heading straight for them. Trev realized that the moment he reached the rear of the shack behind which they were concealed he would see them and sound the alarm.

McTigue said softly, "Hold this animal, Buchman."

Before Trev could make reply McTigue had walked away from him and right out into the open. Trev took the gun from his holster and held it in readiness, wondering what the bounty hunter was up to.

McTigue was not trying to conceal himself now. He was out in the open, although it was still dark back off the street. As the rider approached, McTigue said tersely, "Sounded like I heard somethin' up ahead here. Come easy."

The rider moved up a little faster, not recognizing the voices as McTigue was speaking in gruff tones.

"Where?" the Box B man growled. "I'm tellin' Reynolds they both skipped to hell out."

"One of 'em did, that's sure," McTigue said.

Trev was watching them from a distance of less than twenty feet. He noticed that McTigue was quite close to the rider now .

"Where's the other one?" the Box B man said glumly.

"Here." McTigue chuckled, and Trev saw him suddenly jump up and drag the Box B rider from the saddle, at the same time slashing at his head with the barrel of his pistol.

The rider fell from the saddle and lay still on the ground. McTigue dragged him into the shed, and then the said to Trev, "Reckon you got a horse now, Buchman. Let's move."

Trev went up into the saddle, and the two men shot out into the street, heading south toward Mexican Pass. They could hear someone shouting behind them, and one shot followed.

"Only three of 'em left," McTigue laughed. "They ain't comin' after us."

They rode hard for a mile or so, and then Trev saw his gray along the side of the trail, and he pulled over to change mounts.

When they were entering the pass Trev said to McTigue. "You got me out of a hole. I'm obliged."

"You might have to pay it back some day." McTigue grinned.

"I never found out who you were tailing, either," Trev observed.

"Reckon you might find out about that some day, too."
McTigue laughed. "This ain't the time, Buchman."

It was past one o'clock in the morning when they
reached Rawdon, and Charlie Brackett was waiting peevishly for Trev in the hotel lobby.

"Where in hell you been?" he demanded. "Figured a
bushwhacker got you when you didn't turn up."

"Rode over to Carney," Trev explained. What's happened here?"

"Happened?" Charlie laughed mirthlessly. "Ain't nothin'
much happened, exceptin' that Wes Hampton was burned
out early tonight, an' Tom Caldwell an' his sons are back
at their ranch. Tom was in here today, an' he says they'll
have to kill him to git him off his land now, which is what
they'll do."

Trev frowned. "They burned out Hampton," he murmured.

"Reynolds must of figured Wes was the man tryin' to
organize the ranchers in the basin. They went for him,
first. Must be a dozen hardcase riders came through here
today, headin' out to Box B."

Trev started up to his room, Charlie following him. He
said over his shoulder, "Ben Walters done anything?"

"What in hell can Ben do?" Charlie asked. "Ain't nobody able to prove Reynolds was behind the raid at
Hampton's."

"He wasn't with them," Trev murmured. "Reynolds
was up in Carney gunning for me."

Little Charlie stared at him as they entered Trev's
room. "What happened?" he asked.

Trev told him briefly of Tug Andrews, and of the fight
outside the saloon, and then of the timely arrival of Mc-
Tigue.

Charlie whistled softly after Trev had finished. "Then
it was Reynolds got him," he scowled. "I figured it wasn't
an accident." He paused and then he said, "So where in
hell does that put Ivy Buchman?"

Trev shook his head as he sat down on the edge of the
bed. "I don't like it," he said bitterly.

"Hate like hell to think she was in with Reynolds on it,"
Charlie growled, "but it don't look good. She's got Box B,
an' she's ridin' over everybody to make it bigger. You still
can't prove Reynolds killed Jim 'cause Tug Andrews is
dead."

"Reynolds shot Andrews because Andrews knew," Trev said. "Now I know."

"What do you figure on doin'?"

"I'm killing Reynolds on sight," Trev said, and he pulled off his boots and went to bed.

In the morning Ben Walters called on Trev as he was shaving, and he said quietly, "Have something to show you, Trev. Want to come down?"

Trev looked at the sheriff of Rawdon as he wiped the lather from his face. Walters' jaws were set tight, and there was a glint in his gray eyes.

"Trouble?" Trev asked him.

"Trouble." Walters nodded.

They walked down the street together, and Walters turned into the alley leading back to the Emerald Stables. A small crowd of men were gathered around a buckboard which had been pulled over to one side, the horses taken out of the traces.

The body of a man lay in the back of the buckboard, his boots protruding, and a blanket thrown over him. Walters pushed his way through, Trev following him, and then he pulled the blanket back.

Neil Torrance, the lawyer, lay there, blood on his shirt front where several bullets had gone through him, and a hole in his forehead. The blood on his shirt had dried, and the hole in his forehead had hardly bled at all.

"Rider found the team and the buckboard off the road which leads out to Box B," Walters said laconically. "Must have happened yesterday."

He replaced the blanket and then said to the coroner, "That's it, Bud."

They walked back to the hotel again, and Walters said, "What do you think?"

Trev Buchman didn't have to think about it; he knew. He said quietly, "Torrance told me about a man named Tug Andrews who had seen Lace Reynolds kill my brother."

Walters frowned. "Jim's death was supposed to be an accident," he said.

"He was clubbed from behind," Trev told him evenly, "and knocked unconscious into that corral. The stock was started milling around, and they did the rest."

Ben Walters stared up the street. "What can you prove?" he asked.

"Reynolds shot Andrews over in Carney last night," Trev said. "Is that proof?"

Walters shook his head. "I could lock Reynolds up," he said, "and hold him for a court trial, but how far would I get with that? Every one of Reynolds' riders will testify that he wasn't anywhere near Carney last night."

"I don't figure on going to court with it," Trev murmured.

Walters looked at him for a moment and then he said tersely, "Hell to pay in Cannon Basin these days. You hear Hampton was burned out, and he's lining up all the ranchers to fight Box B?"

"Heard it," Trev nodded. "You have a range war on your hands, Sheriff."

"Reckon I'll ride out to Box B today and have a talk with Ivy Buchman," Walters said. "She might listen to reason."

"Not if she was in with Reynolds on the death of Jim," Trev said bitterly.

Ben Walters scowled and said no more on the subject. When he left, Trev went in for his breakfast. As he ate he saw McTigue sunning himself on the porch of the hotel, and he wondered again at this strange man who liked gunplay, who captured or killed for money, and who had befriended him on more than one occasion.

McTigue had evidently come here searching for someone he was remaining in the vicinity. He would sit on the porch, or stand at bars, and he would listen and say nothing, and then he would take his solitary rides, and when the time was ripe he would go into action. And according to the stories he did not often lose his man. Somewhere in Cannon Basin, someone had a price on his head, and McTigue aimed to collect that money.

Finishing his breakfast, Trev came out just in time to see Ivy Buchman riding brazenly down the street. Seeing him on the walk, she turned her dappled gray in his direction. She made a trim figure on the horse, her tawny hair pulled back away from her forehead, hatless. wearing the same white blouse and the tan riding pants he'd seen her wear before.

Across the road McTigue watched them idly, a cigar in his mouth, and Trev wondered what he was thinking.

Ivy pulled up the horse and said, "You're still around, brother."

Trev nodded. "My town," he said.

"You get around," she told him, and he wondered if she were referring to his trip to Carney the previous night.

"What brings you to town?" he asked. "You lose a friend?"

Ivy Buchman stared at him, the hatred beginning to come to her amber eyes. He realized, then, that she was dangerous, as dangerous as a tigress.

"I understand Neil Torrance was shot," she said evenly. "He was a friend."

"Ben Walters was going to ride out to see you," Trev said. "Save him the trip by stopping in his office."

"About Torrance?" she asked. "I don't know anything about his death."

"About your cutthroat crew riding about Cannon Basin burning people out," Trev told her tersely, "or didn't you know they were doing that."

"Reynolds handles my crew," Ivy snapped. "If he finds men trespassing on Box B land he's getting them off."

"Even if he has to kill them?" Trev asked.

"They take their chances after they've been warned," Ivy told him.

"These men have families," Trev said. "They've been living on the land a long time. A lot of them had permission from my father."

"Your father doesn't own Box B any more," Ivy said viciously.

"Nor my brother," Trev told her significantly, and he saw her turn deathly pale at the statement.

Without a word she lifted her riding whip and brought it down across his face. The hard, burning sting of it brought tears to Trev's eyes as he stepped back, but he disdained even putting his hand up to the welt which had been raised across his left cheek and chin.

Ivy Buchman cut at the dappled gray with the whip and rode off. Trev crossed to the hotel, and as he came up on the porch, McTigue said to him, "She's rough, Buchman. You cross her?"

"I crossed her," Trev nodded, "and it's only the beginning."

"Can't fight a woman," McTigue grinned. "Not you, anyway."

Trev went on up to his room, conscious of the fact that

he would not be fighting a woman in Cannon Basin. He would be fighting evil, evil incarnate.

Coming downstairs a while later, Trev saw that McTigue was still in his chair. He said to Trev, "She saw Walters an' then rode out. There's no talkin' to a woman like that."

"Didn't think he'd get anywhere with her." Trev scowled.

McTigue was looking up the street. He said idly, "You didn't know this gal before she married your brother?"

"Never met her till I got here," Trev told him. He fingered the welt on his cheek, and he added, "I don't want to see her again, either."

"Hard one to handle," McTigue murmured. "Ought to try the other one, Buchman."

Trev looked at him, and then headed up the street to the Wyoming Belle. He wished that McTigue would stop reading his mind.

Rhoda Greene was having luncheon in her rooms above the saloon when Trev asked for her, and she immediately sent word down for him to join her. He went up the back stairs and knocked on the door.

Rhoda had her red hair done up differently this noon, and she wore a simple brown dress with white trim. She had a warm smile for him as she opened the door and said, "Come in, Trev."

Trev took off his hat as he entered the room. It was tastefully furnished. There were rugs on the floor and curtains at each window. As he sat down at a table she poured him coffee from a heavy silver pot which undoubtedly was an heirloom.

"You make good coffee," he said as he caught a whiff of the brown liquid.

"One of my small accomplishments." Rhoda smiled. She sat down across from him and said, "Tell me why Ivy Buchman horsewhipped you. It was a cheap thing to do."

Trev shrugged. "Had it coming, I guess, the way she looks at things," he said. "I asked her to go easy on the ranchers in the basin. She didn't like that, and other things I told her."

"A man is a fool to make an enemy of a woman," Rhoda observed. "Women never forget an injury."

"Jim was a fool to marry her if he could have had you," Trev said, "but maybe it's none of my business."

"We were never serious," Rhoda told him. "I liked Jim. I think he liked me. That was as far as it went, and then he went away and he met Ivy."

Trev sipped his coffee. "How did Jim get along with her?" he asked. "He ever come in and talk to you about it?"

Rhoda hesitated. "It was confidential, of course," she said, "but Jim did stop in now and then for a drink, and he spoke to me. She was giving him a pretty hard time of it very shortly after they were married."·

"How far would she go to get Box B?" Trev asked slowly.

Rhoda looked at him across the table. "I don't know her that well," she said.

Trev put the coffee cup down. "This much I found out in Carney last night," he said. "Jim didn't fall into that corral from a dizzy spell."

Rhoda Greene didn't say anything for a moment. She sat there looking across at him, the trouble in her eyes.

"They'll cut you down, Trev," she said.

"I'll take a lot of cutting," Trev growled.

Both of them heard someone coming up the stairs very fast, and then there was a heavy knock on the door. Outside, Charlie Brackett was calling, "Trev—Trev Buchman?"

Trev opened the door. "All right, Charlie," he said.

Little Charlie was panting from his exertions. He said rapidly, "Wes Hampton's roundin' up a few of the boys. They're ridin' up to Caldwell's place on White Creek."

"Caldwell?" Trev repeated.

"Some of Reynolds' dogs have Tom an' his boys pinned down up there," Charlie Brackett said grimly. "They ain't comin' out alive unless a bunch of us get to hell up there pretty quick. I'm ridin'. Figured you'd like to know about it."

Trev went back to the table for his hat, and then hitched at his gunbelt. He looked at Rhoda on the other side of the table. She'd heard Charlie's message, but she'd said nothing.

"Riding with you," Trev said to Brackett.

"Be careful, Trev," Rhoda Greene told him.

Her hand was resting on the table as she spoke to him, and Trev reached out and touched the hand. She gave him a smile which was filled with promise, and for the first time in his life, riding into trouble, Trev Buchman wished that he'd come back. He had something to come back to now.

Chapter Twelve

W ES HAMPTON and several other men were out in front of the Cheyenne Saloon when Trev hurried up with Charlie Brackett. Hampton was saying heatedly, "We go after this bunch now or they take us one by one. Yesterday they got me; now they're shooting up Tom Caldwell; tomorrow, it'll be you."

"Stop the damn talkin'," Charlie Brackett cut in, "an' let's ride, Wes."

Hampton's eyes lit up when he saw Trev. He said, "You're in this, Trev?"

"I'm in it," Trev nodded. "How many men can you count on?"

"Six here," Hampton told him. "We can pick up more in the basin. One of our boys is riding out now to talk it up."

Trev looked across the street at McTigue sitting on the hotel porch in his favorite chair. McTigue was smoking a cigar, and when Trev looked at him he shook his head gently and grinned, indicating that this was not his fight. Either that, or he didn't like the odds. Peaceful ranchers were going up against seasoned gunmen. With the bounty hunter, Trev realized, it was not a matter of right or justice. McTigue used his gun in matters of self-interest, or for the high dollar, or occasionally because of peculiar likes or dislikes.

"Where's Ben Walters?" Trev asked suddenly.

"He had a talk with Ivy Buchman," Hampton told him, "and then he said he was riding out to Box B. Reckon he wanted to see Reynolds, too."

"Ivy go with him?" Trev asked.

"Still in town," Hampton said.

Charlie Brackett had gone for his own and Trev's horse. He came down the street now, leading Trev's gray, and Trev went up into the saddle. The eight riders clattered out of town, taking the road out to Box B before branching up toward White Creek, and Tom Caldwell's place.

Two miles out of town they picked up a rancher by the name of Shannon, who'd already been warned off by Reynolds' crew. Shannon was ready to ride, and he had one of his crew with him.

It was a mile beyond Shannon's place when Trev, moving at the head of the column of riders, saw the buckskin horse grazing along the edge of a small stream known as Pebble Creek. The buckskin was saddled, and the reins were not trailing as they would have been had the horse been set out to graze by the rider.

"Hells bells!" Charlie Brackett said. "That's Ben Walters' animal."

They found the sheriff of Rawdon a hundred yards down the trace, face down in the grass, the back of his vest bloody. His hat lay to one side, and his gun wasn't out of the holster.

"Bushwhacked," Wes Hampton grated.

Trev bent down to roll the man over. He saw Walters' gray eyes flutter. The man was still alive. Trev cut away the vest and shirt and discovered the wound. It was in the right shoulder, the bullet having gone clean through, making another hole on the other side.

Hastily, he bound up the wound with strips of his shirt, and then Trev assigned one of the men to take Walters back to Rawdon for care. He had become conscious by now, but he still seemed dazed.

Charlie Brackett brought up the sheriff's buckskin, and they lifted him into the saddle, tying him with his rope. He was able to ride, being supported by the other rider, and they started the slow trek back to Rawdon.

Wes Hampton said grimly as they moved west again. "Reckon when you want to make real trouble best thing is to put the law out of the way first. There's nobody to fall back on now, boys. You fight or you're dead."

As they swung north off the Box B trace and headed up toward White Creek, they picked up two more ranchers, along with two of their riders who were anxious to get into the fight. There were thirteen now in the crew that rode out to help Caldwell and his sons in their fight against Reynolds' gunslingers.

Trev wondered as they rode if Caldwell were still holding out. The story had it that they were pinned inside their ranch house and making a fight. He assumed the Caldwell clan had plenty of ammunition. Tom Caldwell would

have been a damned fool not to have stocked up, knowing
that trouble was imminent. He wished, though, that Caldwell and his sons had been smart enough to remain out of
the basin until the law or a group like this had been able
to act, but then Caldwell was protecting his home. He had
a right to be where he was.

Nearing White Creek an hour after leaving Rawdon,
they could hear gunshots in the distance, and Charlie
Brackett said gleefully, "Reckon they're still holdin' out,
Trev. It'll be a fight."

Trev wondered how much of a fight it would be if all
of Reynolds' crew were here. He was hoping against hope
that Lace had only sent half a dozen or so of his gunmen
up to White Creek.

Hampton said to Trev, "Reckon you can handle this
better than I can, Trev. You give the boys orders."

Trev was willing. Someone had to handle a bunch of
men like this, and Hampton obviously wasn't capable.

"We'll move up easily and find out where they're located," Trev said. "When we're ready, we'll hit them."

They rode another half-mile, and then Trev gave the
order for the band to wait, while he moved on ahead
with Charlie Brackett. Caldwell's ranch lay just over the
next ridge. The firing had stopped now, and Charlie said
worriedly, "You figure they broke in, Trev?"

"We'll see," Trev murmured.

Dismounting, they went up on foot to the brow of the
ridge. Down below, backed up against White Creek, lay
Caldwell's ranch. There was no movement about the
house. Several horses, unnerved by the shooting, were
moving about restlessly in the corral.

"Don't see a damned thing," Charlie whispered.

Trev studied the surrounding area carefully, and then
he saw a movement on a slope about a hundred yards
distant. A man was crawling forward on his stomach, us-
ing several big rocks on the slope for protection, and dragging a rifle with him.

"There's another one," Charlie murmured. He pointed
toward a second man farther down the grade.

As Trev watched, the second man opened up with his
Winchester, the bullet knocking more glass from one of
the battered windows in the house below. An answering

shot came from the house, and Charlie said happily, "Old Tom's still makin' a fight of it, Trev."

Several more rifles opened up on the house, and Trev carefully counted the guns.

"Only six of 'em," Charlie said. "Reckon we're in luck, Trev."

"I don't see Reynolds with them," Trev murmured. "I'd like to take some of this bunch to Rawdon and lock them up in Ben Walters' jailhouse. This is a raid on a man's home over a matter which should be settled in court."

"An' they don't have Neil Torrance workin' for them any more," Charlie observed. "It might go a little hard on Ivy Buchman if she took this down to Grant City."

"Go back," Trev ordered, "and bring up the other boys on foot. Spread them out behind Reynolds' crew along the top of this ridge. Tell them not to open fire until I start from this point."

"We knew where the hell their horses were," Charlie observed, "wouldn't be any of 'em gettin' away, Trev."

Trev had had the same thought, and he pointed now to a grove of trees along the bank of the creek, east of the house.

"They could have hidden them in there and circled around the house so that they could shoot down on it from this point. I'll have a look while you're gone, Charlie."

"Be damned careful," Charlie warned. "This crowd don't have no use for you to begin with."

Trev nodded and smiled. When Charlie moved back down the ridge to his horse he made another study of the surrounding territory, deciding again that the grove was the only logical place to conceal half a dozen horses. Studying the grove carefully, he thought he saw movement among the trees.

The guns were beginning to bang along the slope again as the Box B riders sent more lead through Tom Caldwell's shattered windows. Three guns responded from the house, but the Box B men were well concealed behind rocks on the slope, and the answering lead kicked up dust harmlessly.

One man had worked himself down until he was behind one of the outhouses, and less than thirty yards from the main house, From this point he could throw lead through any of the front windows of the house, making it very difficult for those inside to fire at the other men on the slope.

Trev backed away from the ridge and ran down the grade to his horse. He could see Charlie Brackett riding away fast to bring up the other ranchers, and he hoped that they arrived before the Box B men made a concerted dash on the Caldwells.

Leaping into the saddle, Trev moved the gray in a wide circle, coming up on the rear of the grove along the creek. As he rode in among the trees he caught a glimpse of horses, and he knew that he'd been right.

Dismounting, then, he came forward on foot, untying the six horses and then leading them back toward the other end of the grove. The shooting was still going on down at the house as he left the grove and circled back around the ridge, keeping a hill between himself and the ranch.

When he reached the spot from which he'd started, Charlie Brackett and the ranchers were coming up, dismounting at the base of the ridge, and then running forward on foot. Most of them carried Winchesters, and they looked determined as they came up the grade.

Charlie Brackett was grinning in delight when he saw the horses Trev had taken from the grove.

"All we need now," he chuckled, "is them damned riders, Trev. Let's get 'em."

"Spread out," Trev ordered. "work in behind the Box B men. I'll open fire and tell them to give up. They'll make a run for the grove. I want five men over in that direction to head them off when they make the break. We're taking prisoners, and maybe all of them."

Wes Hampton took five men with him and moved over in the direction of the grove. The remaining men fanned out along the brow of the ridge, still keeping back out of sight.

Trev waited until they were all in position, and then he lined his own Winchester at a spot a few feet ahead of the nearest Box B man down the grade. When he squeezed gently on the trigger, a spout of dirt rose in front of the rock where the Box B rider was concealed.

Lifting his voice, Trev yelled, "Every man in this bunch is covered. Throw down your guns and walk up this way real slow."

The Box B men were now caught between two fires. If they remained where they were, they could be shot down by the men above. If they broke for cover, both Trev's men, and Caldwell and his sons could open up on them.

"Who the hell is that?" the Box B man rasped.

"Buchman," Trev said. "You know me. Throw down the guns."

They still didn't know how many men he had with him, so they were hesitating.

Trev called down the ridge, "Hold up your fire, Caldwell. We have all of them from the rear."

Reynolds' gunhands weren't quitting so easily, however. The man to whom Trev had been speaking yelled suddenly, "Back to the trees."

He threw a quick shot at Trev and broke into a run. Trev's Winchester cracked again, and the runner tumbled to the ground, clutching at his leg, rolling over and over in agony.

Trev called up to Charlie Brackett, "Give them some lead, Charlie. Keep it high."

Charlie and the men with him sent several shots over the heads of the men down below, and those who were about to run thought better of it.

"Throw down the guns," Trev ordered, "and move up here. If we open up you'll be dead in two minutes."

They recognized the truth of this. First one man, and then a second, dropped his gun. The Box B man who had been down at the outhouse, hearing the shots and seeing what was going on, made a break for the grove.

He'd covered about twenty-five yards when a shot from one of Hampton's men knocked him down. Trev watched him roll and come up to a sitting position, clutching at his left shoulder, and it was two down, and four still up.

"Walk easy," Trev ordered.

The Box B men came up the grade then, leaving their guns behind. Tom Caldwell and his two sons burst out of the house, yelling, when they realized the fight was over.

Trev gave the order to look after the two wounded men, and then he had Charlie Brackett bring up the horses he'd taken from the grove.

Wes Hampton came running up, puffing, his round face red.

"We stopped them." he yelled.

"This is only part of them," Trev told him.

"You got no right bustin' into this, Buchman," one of the Box B men hissed. "Reynolds gave us orders to run this hombre across the creek. He's on Box B land now."

"A court will have to decide that," Trev told him. "In the meantime you men are under arrest for attacking a man in his own house. We'll see what Sheriff Walters has to say about this."

"How long you think we'll stay there, mister?" the Box B man sneered.

He was a tall, thin man with a drooping shoulder and long black Indian hair.

"Maybe this town will get wise and lynch the bunch of you," Trev said, "before Reynolds can get you out."

He had a look at the two wounded men. The man he'd shot down had a bullet through the calf of his leg and wasn't feeling too good about it. The second man had taken a piece of lead through the left shoulder. Both men would need a doctor's care back in town.

Tom Caldwell and his two sons came up the hill, shaking hands with everybody in sight. He said to Trev. "Reckon you was right that I should of stayed away a mite longer, but I couldn't see these dogs takin' my place, Trev. I put a heap of work in this spread."

"Hope you can hold it," Trev told him. "I were you I'd clear out, though, if they came again. I'd wait till the court acted."

"We have to fight 'em together," Wes Hampton was saying enthusiastically. "You see what the bunch of us can do?"

Trev didn't say anything to that. Fighting together was a wonderful thing for an army of men. This was not an army; these men were ranchers with families, and now that this little affair was over they would have to get back to their chores. Lace Reynolds' Box B men remained intact. They could strike everywhere. They were in a sense a small, compact army.

Today, the ranchers had been fortunate. Without any real effort or gunplay, they'd had the Box B men at a disadvantage. The next time it might be different, and there would be widows in black in Rawdon.

Trev had the two wounded men carried to a buckboard Tom Caldwell provided, and the ranchers headed back toward Rawdon with their four prisoners. They were going back to a town, Trev Buchman remembered, without a sheriff, and it was not going to be a pleasant town, particularly for him.

Chapter Thirteen

IT WAS LATE AFTERNOON, almost dusk, when they rode into Rawdon. Trev had the prisoners herded into the empty prison cells, after Doc Waterbury had tended to the two wounded men.

A crowd had gathered at the jailhouse, and they were still there as Trev left with the keys to visit Ben Walters, who was in bed in his rooms at a boardinghouse down the street.

He found the law man fully conscious, but pale and weak, his shoulder bandaged.

"Hear you had a little excitement up at White Creek," he said as Trev came in.

"Had some yourself," Trev observed. "See who got you, Ben?"

Walters shook his head grimly. "Heard the shot. I was knocked down. That's all I remember."

"I have six prisoners for you." Trev smiled and jangled the keys in his hand.

"I have a proposition for you," Walters told him quietly, and Trev thought he knew what it was.

"Go ahead," he said.

"Either have me carried down to that jailhouse the way I am, and set me up in front of those cells," Walters said, "or pin that star on yourself."

He nodded to the silver badge on the dresser next to the bed.

"How am I in this?" Trev asked.

"This used to be your town," Walters told him. "You said you've worn the star before. Why not wear it here?"

Trev looked down at the wounded man. "You know Reynolds has to come in to get his boys out of your jailhouse," he said.

"I know it." Walters nodded. "I wish to hell I could help you."

Trev picked up the star and fingered it thoughtfully.

"Reckon you know there's nobody else in this town will wear it," Ben Walters told him, "with Box B running loose the way they are. Before any of these boys can get a case in court, they'll all be wiped out, and a lot of 'em dead. After that it won't matter."

"I can't stop Reynolds alone," Trev pointed out.

"Deputize anybody you want," Walters told him.

Trev smiled. "Maybe Charlie Brackett," he said. "Who else would go along with me?"

"A lot of 'em went out today," Walters observed.

"That was different," Trev said. "You wear the star and you're high on the fence. Anybody can knock you off."

Ben Walters looked up at the ceiling. "Reckon we can drop it, then," he said. "Those boys will be out of the cells in twenty-four hours, and Box B will ride herd all over Cannon Basin with nobody to stop 'em."

Trev pinned the star on his shirt. "Swear me in, Ben," he said.

He left the room a few minutes later, and walked back toward the jailhouse. Charlie Brackett and a few of the ranchers were still there, a little confused, not knowing what they were supposed to do next. Most of the crowd had dispersed.

When Charlie saw the star on Trev's vest he grinned and said, "Figured Ben would rope you in on that."

"I need a deputy," Trev said. "Are you it, Charlie?"

"Sign me up, Trev."

Trev swore him in, and then went back to have a look at the prisoners. The two wounded men had been put in a separate cell, and Doc Waterbury had worked over them and bandaged the wounds, making them as comfortable as possible. The other four men were in the second cell.

"How long you figure you can keep us here?" the tall Box B man rasped at Trev as he went by.

"Till you rot," Trev told him.

"Be lookin' you up, mister," the tall man murmured, "when we get out."

Trev ignored him as he went back to the office, and then told Charlie that he was going back to the hotel to make arrangements for sending food over to the prisoners.

When he was coming back, McTigue signaled to him from the porch of a nearby saloon. Trev pulled up, standing on the walk below.

McTigue took the cigar from his mouth and said casually, "They're layin' eight to three inside that you won't live more than forty-eight hours, Buchman. What do you think of that?"

"I'd take some of that money," Trev told him.

"You're a damned fool," McTigue said, and he sounded almost irritable. "How in hell you let Walters talk you into wearin' that star?"

"Somebody had to wear it," Trev stated.

"Somebody didn't want to live long." McTigue scowled. "Wouldn't surprise me if Reynolds came here tonight an' had a showdown with you."

"I'll be waiting for him," Trev said. He smiled and added, "I could use more deputies, McTigue. You like to wear a star, too?"

McTigue shook his head. "Reckon I don't like the odds," he said. "Besides, I never work for the law."

Trev said softly, "Lace Reynolds the man you're after, McTigue?"

McTigue smiled down at him. "Never said who I was after, mister," he murmured.

"Over in Carney the other night," Trev told him, "I had your gun on my side. Can I count on it tonight or some other night against Reynolds?"

McTigue shrugged. "Depends on the odds," he said, "an' on how I feel at the time. I don't figure on gettin' shot up just to protect some damn fool's wearin' a tin star on his shirt."

Trev just laughed and went on down to the jailhouse. A half-hour later two boys from the hotel kitchen came over with supper for all of them, and ate with Charlie Brackett in the office.

They were finishing up when Ivy Buchman stormed into the room. It was past seven o'clock in the evening now, and she wore a jacket and a hat, and Trev noticed that she was again carrying her riding whip.

"I understand you have some of my men in here," Ivy snapped.

Trev said to Charlie Brackett, "Have a look outside, Charlie."

"I didn't bring anybody with me," Ivy told him grimly, "yet."

Charlie Bracket grinned and went out, wiping his mouth with the back of his sleeve.

Trev said, "Your men are in the cells in the back if you wish to see them."

"I want them released," Ivy told him.

"They were attacking a man in his own home," Trev stated. "They're being held till the circuit judge arrives in two weeks, and they'll go on trial, then."

Ivy came up closer to him, gripping the whip tightly in her hand so that the knuckles showed white.

"You think you can keep them here?" she grated.

"Don't use that whip again," Trev warned her.

In reply she slashed at his face again, but this time he was expecting it and he had his arm raised to take the blow. He grabbed at her right wrist holding the whip, and then he slammed her back hard against the wall of the room, twisting her right hand so that the whip fell to the floor.

He held her there for one moment, his face inches from hers, and she stared at him, her eyes almost yellow in color, and then they softened up, and she smiled, and said.

"It didn't have to be this way, Trev. This wasn't what I had planned."

He realized that if he wanted to, even now, he could kiss her, and she would respond. She was staring up into his face, smiling, her eyes wide, lips slightly parted.

"Trev," she said softly. "Trev, I'll get rid of Reynolds. I'll—"

He pushed her away roughly. She'd gotten rid of Neil Torrance; possibly, she'd gotten rid of Jim; she got rid of everybody when she was finished with them.

"Get out," he said without looking at her. "Get out."

"I'll kill you for this, Trev," she said softly. "Do you hear me? I'll kill you for this."

He was positive that if she'd had a gun on her she would have carried out the threat then and there.

"Get out," he told her again, and this time she left.

Charlie Brackett came back in and said, "Don't see any Box B riders around. She come in alone."

"Finish your coffee," Trev told him.

"She's a bad one," Charlie murmured. "Always said she was a bad one. Jim brought himself a peck of trouble when he brought her home."

"He found her back East?" Trev asked. "Chicago?"

"Hell," Charlie said. "Could of been Cheyenne. Jim

never said much about it. She don't look like no real Eastern gal to me. Jim went East to buy some prize bulls. He come home with Ivy."

Trev didn't say anything to that. He was finishing his own coffee when McTigue stuck his head in the door to impart some information.

"Four hardcases just come off the train." McTigue grinned. "Maybe they're just lookin' the town over, an' maybe Reynolds brought 'em in. Figured you'd like to know."

"We're obliged." Trev scowled.

"Reckon Reynolds should be ridin' in here any hour now with the rest of his crew," McTigue went on. "Why in hell don't you boys get wise an' open the cell doors, an' then head for the hills yourselves."

"That all you have to say?" Trev asked him.

"Best advice you'll ever have in this world," the bounty hunter chuckled, "an' maybe the last. Get the hell out. It's not your fight, Buchman."

Trev pointed to the star on his shirt. "Now it's my fight," he said.

"Where in hell are your friends?" McTigue wanted to know. "These ranchers backin' you when Reynolds, an' his crew, an' these hardcases come lookin' you up for a showdown?"

"I don't know who's backing me up," Trev said.

"I'll tell you who," McTigue snapped. "Nobody. This crowd you had with you today are all headin' out to their ranches. You two boys are sittin' ducks."

Trev shrugged. "We had your gun on our side," he observed, "it would even things up more."

Charlie Brackett was grinning, but McTigue said sourly, "When I'm ready to die, mister, I'm dyin' for myself, an' not for some chicken-hearted cowmen shouldn't be buckin' men like Reynolds in the first place."

He went out, then, and Charlie laughed and said, "Sounds like he's a little peeved, Trev. You figure he's tryin' to scare us off with the talk about four more hardcases?"

"You run these dishes back to the hotel," Trev told him, "and then have a look around. You'll know strangers in town when you see them."

"Reckon I'll know them," Charlie nodded. "See if Reynolds' boys are comin' in, too."

When Charlie had gone out, Trev checked over his gun carefully. He was putting it back in the holster when there was a knock on the door, and when he opened it, Rhoda Greene stood there.

"Come in," he said.

She was wearing a shawl on her head, and she took it off when she came in. He saw her eyes move to the star on his shirt as she said, "Trev, there's going to be trouble tonight. I hear the talk."

He smiled down at her and said, "You came to warn me about it?"

"I wouldn't like to see anything happen to you, Trev," she said.

She was looking at him steadily, standing very close to him, her dark eyes shining. Beyond in the cells and out of sight, Trev could hear the Box B men talking in low tones. One of the wounded men was cursing at the pain in his body.

Stepping forward, Trev put his arms around the girl and drew her close. He kissed her gently, and then he looked down into her face, and she was smiling, and there were tears in her eyes.

"What's that for, Trev?" she asked him softly.

"If I come out of this," Trev told her, "I'd like to try to make a go of it with you. I don't have much to offer but I'll get started somewhere."

"I have my place," Rhoda told him. "I can sell it."

He kissed her again, then, and he said, "We'll talk about it in the morning."

Then he realized that there was a very good chance that he would not be alive in the morning. A man like McTigue, who weighed the odds very carefully, was telling him to get out of it.

For the moment, Trev stood there, tempted. The ranchers in Cannon Basin were not his business. They'd taken their chances when they'd moved in on Bull Buchman's range, even if he hadn't bothered to chase them out, and Jim had been lax. It was their own responsibility to get out as best they could, but getting out would leave Ivy Buchman and Lace Reynolds in charge, and Lace had killed Jim. Trev Buchman couldn't ride away from that.

"I—I'm afraid about tonight, Trev," Rhoda said.

"You want me to walk out of it?"

She looked at him steadily. "I want what you want,"

she said. "I don't want you to regret something all of your life, Trev."

"I'll have to stay," Trev told her.

"I thought you would." Rhoda nodded. "Promise me you won't take any unnecessary risks, Trev."

"I'll be dead if I do." Trev smiled. "Reckon you'd better get back now."

He opened the door for her, and she held his hand for a moment, looking at him, and then she left. Trev walked back to the desk and sat on the edge of it for a moment, staring down at the floor. Then he walked back to the last cell to have a look at his wounded prisoners, and he was cursed roundly for his trouble.

He came back to find Charlie Brackett in the office, a frown on his face. He sat down in the sheriff's chair behind the desk and said grimly, "Reckon they're here, Trev. Four of 'em in the Cheyenne Saloon. Never seen any of 'em before. All wearin' their guns low, an' talkin' little. One of 'em asked where he could find Lace Reynolds."

"What about Reynolds?" Trev asked.

"He ain't in town, yet, from what I can see," Charlie told him.

"Keep outside," Trev ordered. "We want to know when Reynolds rides in."

"Gonna be a hell of a lot of 'em," Charlie muttered.

"You like to ride out, Charlie?" Trev asked.

"Not me," the little man said promptly.

Trev looked down at him and smiled. "What are you fighting for, Charlie?" he asked curiously.

Charlie Brackett thought for a moment. "Damned if I know," he confessed. "I got no use fer Reynolds for one thing, but that ain't reason enough to get my head shot off."

"What about law and order?" Trev asked.

Charlie grinned. "Ain't bothered me much either way," he said. He looked at Trev and said, "Who the hell you fightin', Trev? You ain't gettin' Box B back, an' it don't do you no good to help somebody else chop up that range."

Trev slid off the edge of the desk and walked toward the door to look out.

"I don't like to see one man or one woman get to be top dog," he said, "anywhere, any time, under any condition. It's not good. My father was top dog in Cannon Basin. It wasn't good for him."

Charlie noded. "Reckon if a man's gonna die," he said, "that's as good a reason as any other."

"It'll do for me," Trev murmured.

Chapter Fourteen

IT WAS past ten o'clock in the evening when Charlie Brackett came back to the jailhouse with the word that Lace Reynolds had ridden in with four of his riders.

"Down at the Cheyenne," Charlie said succinctly. "Reckon this is it, Trev. We stayin' here an' waitin' for 'em?"

"We'll circulate outside," Trev told him, and he walked over to the board where the keys for the cells were hanging.

"What about them damned prisoners?" Charlie wanted to know.

Trev took the keys down from the wall and walked over to a pail of water standing in a corner of the room. The pail was painted red and half-filled with murky water for use in case of fire.

Holding the keys just above the water he let them drop out of sight under the water, and then he said, "Anybody watching this building, Charlie?"

"Damned if I know," Charlie confessed. "Reynolds could of sent somebody down here to keep an eye on us."

"You step outside," Trev told him. "I'll move out through this side window into the alley."

"Where we gonna meet?" Charlie wanted to know.

"I'll work my way down to the Fairfax Stables," Trev told him. "I want Reynolds to think I'm still in here."

"He'll be headin' up here," Charlie said. "Reckon we'd best be out, an' give ourselves a little room to move."

Charlie left by the front door, closing it behind him, and then Trev unbolted the barred window and swung it open. One of the prisoners saw him going out through the window, and he called sardonically, "Where the hell you goin', Buchman? It gettin' too hot in here for you?"

Trev just smiled and pulled the grate shut as he let himself down into the alley, and then headed back away from the street. Reaching the rear of the jailhouse, he turned left, passing behind several buildings along the main street until he came to Fairfax Stables. He had to go over a half-broken picket fence here, and when he was stepping over the fence, Charlie called softly, "This way, Trev."

Trev found the little man waiting in the shadows to the right of the stable entrance. He said when Trev came up, "Anybody see you comin' out, Trev?"

"Nobody," Trev told him, and then a gun banged suddenly, and a slug ripped into the wood of the barn, inches from his head.

The flash of the gun came from a spot on the other side of the picket fence, and at a distance of about thirty yards. Trev fired once at the man back there in the darkness, and then, grabbing Charlie's arm, literally jerked him into the stable.

"Reckon you was followed," Charlie said as they ran down toward the rear of the stable.

There were horses in the stalls on both sides of them, and a lantern hung from a nail on one of the overhead beams, providing a dull light. Trev spotted his own gray gelding in one of the stalls as they raced toward the rear door of the stable.

They came out into the open and swung around the corner of the building, heading back toward Main Street. They hadn't taken more than a dozen strides down the alley when they saw a bunch of men come running up from the street.

Someone yelled, and then a shot rang out.

"Get back!" Trev called sharply.

There were at least four men in the alley at the other end, and their guns opened up on them, winking orange in the night. He fired once, and he saw a man drop to his knees, and then he was running, Charlie Brackett with him, keeping close to the wall.

He heard Charlie gasp as they reached the head of the alley and swung around out of range of the bullets. Trev stopped and fired twice back into the alley to keep the Box B men down there, and then he said anxiously to the little puncher, "You all right, Charlie?"

"Picked up a little lead," Charlie muttered. "Keep goin', Trev."

"Not without you," Trev retorted. "Where did you get it, Charlie?"

"Right over the belt," Charlie told him. "On the left side. I ain't runnin' too far, Trev."

He was leaning against the wall of the building, his gun sagging in his hand, as Trev fired down into the alley.

"You move on," Charlie said. "They ain't after me so much anyway, Trev."

"I know where I can take you," Trev said. "Can you walk at all?"

"Move till I drop," Charlie murmured. "Don't hurt, though. Don't hurt a bit, Trev."

Trev held him around the shoulders and started him down along the rear of the buildings on the main street. When he reached the Wyoming Belle, he helped Charlie up on to the loading platform which opened on a storeroom at the back of the saloon, and then he located the door and pushed Charlie inside.

In the darkness he fumbled around until he'd located some of the beer barrels. He sat Charlie Brackett down on one of them. The smell of beer was strong.

"Hold tight," he said. "I'll be back, Charlie."

"Ain't goin' no place," Charlie said softly. "Stayin' right here, Trev."

Trev realized that the little puncher had gone about as far as he could go. This was the end of the trail for him until they could get a doctor to work on his wound.

Locating the door which led out to the bar, Trev opened it, finding himself in a little room behind the bar. One of Rhoda Greene's bartenders was coming back through the entrance way from the bar, and Trev said to him, "Tell Miss Greene I'd like to see her right away."

The bartender nodded and went out. In a few moments Rhoda came through the door, her face pale.

"We heard the shots up the street, Trev," she whispered. "Are you all right?"

"I'm all right," Trev told her. "Charlie Brackett was hit. He's in your storeroom at the back. Can you get him upstairs and then have Doc Waterbury come in."

"I'll take care of Charlie," Rhoda promised. "What about you? Where are you going now?"

Trev grinned. "Last place they'd think to look for me." He chuckled. "My hotel room."

"Can you get over there?" Rhoda asked him.

"They're looking for me in the back alleys," Trev told

her. "I'll walk out the front door and cross to the hotel."

"Hide that star," Rhoda warned him. "It shows up in the night."

Trev nodded and unpinned the star, putting it in his pocket. He kissed her, then, and went out into the barroom.

The Wyoming Belle was almost empty now because everybody had gone out to the street after the shooting stopped. The porch of the saloon was crowded, and several men stood behind the batwing doors, looking out, blocking Trev's way.

He touched one man on the shoulder, and he said, "Going through."

The men stared at him as he went by out onto the porch and through the crowd gathered there. He crossed the road without haste, and as he was halfway across he saw two men run out of a side street and cross to the other side of the road. If they saw him they took no notice of him as he went up on the walk, and then entered the hotel.

The hotel clerk stared at him, too, as he crossed the lobby and went calmly up to his room. He was positive no one on the street would tip off the Box B men as to his location. None of them had any use for Box B, and they were beginning to have their respect for him.

In his room he closed the door, locked it, and then moved to the window which opened on the street. Looking down he could see two men hurrying by on the walk. He had a view of the jailhouse from here, too, but none of Reynolds' men as yet seemed to have made any attempt to free the prisoners. They would have their difficulties trying to break them out because the locks on Ben Walters' cell doors had been very heavy, and they would resist even gunfire.

Trev pulled a chair over to the window and sat down, resting the gun on the window ledge. He'd reloaded after the first flurry of shots, and he was ready for them again as he sat here in the darkness. The purpose now was to throw Reynolds off his guard, keep him confused as to where his man was, and then at the opportune moment, set him up. It was not going to be easy, but then Trev hadn't expected it to be easy when he accepted Ben Walters' star.

He was in the room for about five minutes when he heard a light knock on the door. Moving away from the window, Trev waited against the wall, gun in hand. He was sure that if it were Box B men, they'd have kicked in the door and sprayed the room with lead. He waited, and then he heard a man outside say softly, "Buchman?"

It was McTigue.

Trev moved to the door, turned the key, and opened it, letting McTigue slip inside. He locked the door again behind the bounty hunter and said, "You see me come in here?"

"Everybody saw you come in but Box B," McTigue told him. "You're damned clever, Buchman. You worked with me we could make a fortune."

"Reckon I could use that cover gun tonight." Trev grinned. "You still making a deal, McTigue?"

"Don't need a deal now," McTigue chuckled from the other side of the room.

Trev could see his figure dimly in the darkened room. "How's that?" he asked. "You find your man?"

"Found him," McTigue said casually.

Trev stared at him curiously. "Ready to turn him over?" he asked.

"Not here," McTigue laughed. "Ain't no law in this town right now. Law's on the run."

There was the quick glow of light in the room as McTigue struck a match and touched it to a cigar in his mouth. Trev sat by the window, smelling the cigar, looking down on the street. He wondered who McTigue's man was, but he didn't ask, knowing that McTigue wouldn't tell him.

"How long you figure on staying' here?" the bounty hunter asked.

Trev shrugged. He was still watching the jailhouse, wondering when Reynolds' men would head there to release the prisoners. He knew that they were still searching the back alleys, vacant lots and empty sheds for him probably on both sides of the street now. Reynolds wouldn't give up until he was dead.

"I'll move soon enough," Trev said.

Then he saw four men come out of an alley a few doors down from the jailhouse. They stood for a moment, talking on the walk, and then they started up the empty street in the directon of the jailhouse. When they passed a patch of light from one of the saloons, Trev recognized Lace Reynolds with them. Lace still had a patch of adhesive tape across one cheek from the fight.

"Get ready to move," Trev told McTigue, and then rested the barrel of his six-gun on the sill of the open window, steadied the gun, and squeezed on the trigger. He placed his bullet a few feet ahead of the walking men, and they broke for cover at the sound of the shot.

Reynolds himself darted in through an open doorway, but several of the other men went up on the nearest porch, crouched, and fired up at Trev's window.

He dropped one of them with his second shot, spilling the man down on to the walk, and then he ran for the door. McTigue was standing there, the cigar in his mouth, holding it open for him.

He ran through, and then across the corridor and into one of the rooms on the opposite side of the hallway. More than half of the rooms on the upper floor of the hotel were not taken, and he easily found one with an open door.

Running through to the window that opened on the rear of the house, he yanked open the window and crawled through to drop to the kitchen shed roof several feet below. As he did so, he saw McTigue coming after him, the cigar still in his mouth.

"You in this?" he grinned as the bounty hunter dropped down beside him.

"Hell, I'm not havin' this bunch mistake me for you, an' gettin' shot up."

Trev lowered himself by his hands down from the shed roof, and then dropped the few remaining feet to the ground, McTigue coming after him. They ran left, then, toward the west end of town, keeping back from the light from the buildings along the way.

Back on the main street they could still hear Reynolds' men firing at the window from which the shot had come. In a matter of moments now the Box B men would be coming around to the rear of the hotel, hoping to cut Trev off, and finding him gone, they would have to start their search all over again.

"Where you headin'?" McTigue panted as they ran, stumbling through vacant lots.

"Keep out of sight," Trev told him, "until we're ready to hit at them again."

"How the hell long can your luck hold out?" McTigue growled. "Reckon you're livin' on borrowed time now, mister."

Trev swung down an alley which led again to the main street, and as he approached the street, two men suddenly swerved into the alley and came stumbling up in his direction.

The alley was less than a half-dozen feet wide, making it impossible for him to hide against the wall. Behind him, he heard McTigue curse suddenly. If they turned and ran back the other way, the men coming at them would open fire, knowing who they were.

There was only one other choice, and Trev took it. He'd slackened his speed, but now he started running again, making no effort to conceal himself, even calling back to McTigue to hurry it up.

The two men who'd come into the alley stopped, hearing them coming, and as Trev drew near in the darkness, he said sharply. "You guys get behind that hotel. Watch the rear door."

The two Box B men ran on again, cursing as they stumbled over debris in the alley. Trev waited until McTigue came up, laughing softly.

McTigue said with a chuckle, "You figure a lot of these boys don't even know who in hell they're after. They never even seen him."

"That's it." Trev nodded.

He remembered that there were four hardcases now working with Reynolds who'd only gotten off the train an hour or so ago. They could not be expected to know who they were after.

"What now?" McTigue asked when they came up to the street.

"Still with me?" Trev asked him.

"Duckin' into the first saloon I come to," McTigue told him. "Hell with this chasin' through the alleys."

"You did it before," Trev reminded him, thinking of the night McTigue had deliberately called for a fight with Box B by opening up with his gun from an alley similar to this.

"Odds were better then," McTigue told him. "This

bunch has you in a corner, Trev. You're wearin' the star now, an' you can't ride away from it."

Trev looked out onto the street from the alley. He could ess men watching from saloons, looking out over the doors. No one ventured to come out on the street.

The jailhouse was about thirty yards from where they stood. Another dozen yards beyond was the doorway into which Lace Reynolds had run when the shots came from the hotel window. Trev doubted that Reynolds was still there.

"You figure on gettin' to Reynolds alone?" McTigue asked.

"Only chance I have," Trev told him. "If I knock him down I think it'll be over."

"What about the woman?"

Trev didn't know about Ivy Buchman. He hadn't seen her since he'd practically driven her out of the jailhouse earlier in the evening. He didn't know whether she was still in town, waiting to hear that he'd been killed, or if she'd gone back to Box B.

"She might be tougher than Reynolds," McTigue said dryly. "You ever figure it that way. Buchman?"

"Reynolds first," Trev told him. "He's in this town with a gun on me."

"Her gun," McTigue corrected him. "She runs Box B."

Trev saw a man come out of a side street and cross to the hotel side, and then a second man ran past the alley where he stood with McTigue.

"Where you goin'?" McTigue asked curiously.

"Other side again," Trev said. "Getting too hot here."

Apparently, the Box B men figured he was still in the hotel, or close to it, and they were converging on that point. His quick escape from the hotel had thrown them.

He looked across at the jailhouse, thinking that Lace Reynolds wouldn't look for him there. They knew he'd left the jailhouse to get away from them. And, sooner or later, Reynolds would again be heading for the jailhouse, not expecting to find his man there.

Trev edged out toward the street, and McTigue said behind him, "Cover you this time. After that you're on your own."

Trev lifted a hand in acknowledgment, and then walked calmly toward the jailhouse.

He saw two men running down the street, but their backs were toward him and they didn't see him as he went up on the walk on the opposite side of the street, and then up the two low steps to the sheriff's office.

Pushing in the door, he stepped inside and closed the door behind him. He stood there for a few moments after that, breathing hard, his gun still in his hand, and then he heard one of the Box B men in the cells call, "Lace? Lace Reynolds?"

They couldn't see him from the cells, and they assumed that Reynolds had finally come in to break them out.

Trev stood still, not wanting them to know that he was here and shout the alarm out to Reynolds. He stood where he was, and then he heard another man say, "Somebody come in that door, Tom? Heard it open."

"Must've gone out again," Tom said. "What in hell is Reynolds waitin' for? He knows damned well Buchman ain't in here."

Trev moved one step at a time, crossing the room to his desk, making no noise. When he reached the desk, he sat down in the chair behind it, placing his gun in front of him. He had stopped running now, and it was up to Reynolds to find him.

He was positive that Reynolds would be the first one through the door, and he had to take care of Reynolds. Maybe with Reynolds down, other men in town would swing to his side and make it hot for the Box B gunslingers.

He sat very still behind the desk, listening to the men in the cells talking and grumbling. All of them were angry because Reynolds hadn't already come into the empty jailhouse to break them loose.

A few men went past on the run outside, and Trev could hear their boots on the wood, dying out as they kept going. One of the men in the cells yelled out through the rear window of his cell. "Reynolds, you gettin' us the hell out of here?"

Trev stayed where he was behind the flat-topped desk, facing the door, the gun on the desk in front of him. If Reynolds didn't come in through that door first, it meant that they had him pinned down here, and he'd never get out, unless McTigue and the rest of this town came to his rescue, and he doubted that.

A clock was ticking on the wall nearby, and one of the

wounded men was groaning and mumbling a little. Then Trev heard voices coming closer to the door, and he picked up the gun, cocking the hammer.

"When you comin' in, Reynolds?" one of the prisoners whooped again, and Trev Buchman was glad now that he'd been extra careful coming back into the jailhouse. The men would not be calling for Reynolds to come in and get them out if they knew their guard was waiting with a gun trained on the door.

The voices were coming closer, and then Trev distinctly heard Lace Reynolds say, "You two men head down to the east end of town. Start working back, building by building. Stick together."

Again, Trev heard boots on the walk, and then the door opened and Lace Reynolds came in. The ramrod of Box B walked in without any hesitation. He was closing the door behind him when he saw Trev at the desk and the gun in Trev's hand.

"You want me?" Trev asked him softly.

He gave Reynolds every chance. The Box B man's eyes flicked, but he didn't go for his gun immediately. In that one brief moment of delay, Trev saw the grudging admiration in Reynolds' eyes. Then Reynolds went for his gun, his right hand moving very fast.

He was wearing a Navy Colt, and he brought it out of the holster with great speed. He fired first because he'd figured that Trev wouldn't give him the opportunity to shoot at all, and he fired before the gun was high enough.

The lead gouged into one corner of the desk, and then Trev sent two bullets at the Box B man, both of them taking him in the chest.

Reynolds staggered back against the door. He reached for the door knob as if seeking a way out, and he fumbled for the knob with his left hand, his eyes getting glassy, his gun limp at his side.

Trev watched him as he slid down to a sitting position, and even before his body struck the floor he was dead. Swinging around the desk, Trev darted for the door to slide the big bolt across it.

The men in the cells were yelling, "Reynolds? Lace Reynolds?"

Trev remembered, then, the open window grate out of which he'd climbed less than twenty minutes before. He ran back to close it and then stopped within six feet of the window— Ivy Buchman was standing outside, looking in at him, the gun very steady in her hand.

She stood in a patch of light from the jailhouse lamp, hatless, a wildness in her amber eyes. He realized, then, that she had been looking for him, too, ready to shoot him down like a dog if she had the opportunity.

She had the opportunity now, and it was impossible to miss at that distance. He realized that she had been close to the building, possibly with Reynolds when he'd come up to the jailhouse, and hearing the shots inside, she'd surmised what had happened and had gone immediately to the window.

Trev stood there looking at her, his gun still in his hand, but the muzzle pointing toward the floor. He had, perhaps, a second to live. He didn't think he had much more. He wondered if he would have shot her, even in self-defense, if he'd had the opportunity.

He didn't have the opportunity, though. He had only a second or a fraction of a second to live because Ivy Buchman was going to kill him. He could read that very clearly in her eyes. He had rejected her; he was actively fighting her in her drive to make Box B the biggest spread in this part of the country, and for that too he deserved to die, but he knew that it was primarily because of the rejection. Her pride had been hurt, and it had to be assuaged with blood.

Trev waited for her gun to go off, and then another gun sounded instead, from a point farther back in the alley. The girl with the tawny hair staggered. She dropped the gun which had been lined on Trev's body, and she grasped at the window sill with both hands, staring at him with unseeing eyes.

Then slowly she sagged, dropping out of sight, her hands relinquishing their hold on the window sill.

Trev moved up to the window. Then he turned and ran for the door, throwing it open. Two men were running toward the jailhouse, guns in hand—the two men Reynolds had sent up the street.

Trev dropped one of them with his first shot. He missed with the second shot, and the Box B man leaped into an alley out of range.

Across the road were three other men just emerging from a side street, having heard the firing from the jailhouse. Before Trev could wheel his gun on them, a gun began to sound from the alley, and two of the three men dropped, one man clutching at his leg. The third man had had enough, and he turned and raced back into the street.

McTigue came out of the alley, then, his gun still in his hand, and he said succinctly, "Reckon your fight is over, Buchman."

Trev thought so, too. With Reynolds dead, and at least half of the Box B crew out of the fight, and now with Ivy Buchman shot down, it was doubtful whether the remaining men would wish to continue the fight.

Moving back into the alley, Trev picked up the girl and carried her into the jailhouse.

"Reckon she's dead," McTigue said casually. "She had you covered inside, an' she was aimin' to finish you. Didn't have too much time to think about it."

Trev placed the girl on the floor. She was dead. McTigue's bullet had gone through her side as she stood at the window.

McTigue stood there, looking down at her, and then, a trifle awkwardly, he took off his hat.

"Ain't never shot a woman before," he murmured, "but this'll save me the trouble of bringin' her in."

"Bringing her in?" Trev repeated.

Outside, he could hear people coming into the streets again, and a man was saying, "Mrs. Buchman was shot. Reynolds was shot."

"She's the one I've been after," McTigue explained. "A bank back in Missouri has a thirty-five-hundred-dollar reward out for her, dead or alive. I come up this way to collect."

Trev was staring at the thin man with the bony face. "What was the charge?" he asked.

"She was in with two other hombres," McTigue explained, "in the robbery of this Missouri bank. Seems she set the thing up by livin' in the town for a while. A teller was shot, an' one of the bandits plugged in the chest, too. She an' the other feller got away. Still wonderin' whether it could've been Reynolds. Reckon your brother run into her back East, Chicago or somewhere, when he was there. She had easy pickings when she saw him, an' then she an' Reynolds took over Box B when your brother fell into that corral, or was pushed—one or the other."

"You followed her out here?" Trev asked.

"Picked up her trail back East," McTigue explained. "I move with these posters. Been askin' around, an' waitin' my time. Got a wire this mornin' from a Pinkerton man back East. He'd been trailin' her, an' lost her in Chicago. Told me she'd married a rancher, but didn't know who, or where they'd gone. Described her in his wire, an' there's no doubt it was Ivy."

"You'll collect your money," Trev murmured.

McTigue smiled. "Reckon you won't do so bad yourself, mister," he pointed out.

"How's that?" Trev asked him.

"Box B goes back to you," McTigue told him. "This gal didn't have any relatives that anybody knew."

Trev looked down at the dead girl for a moment, and then he turned and went outside, pushing his way through the crowd around the door. The cool night air felt good on his face. He'd been slightly sickened by the shooting of Ivy Buchman, and it was good to get out in the open again.

McTigue had come outside with him. He was touching a match to a cigar, watching Trev out of the corner of his eye.

Trev said to him, "You figure out how Torrance fitted into this?"

McTigue shrugged. "Torrance knew the law, an' he was crooked. Ivy Buchman an' Reynolds needed a lawyer to make their claims stick in court. Maybe they told him about your brother; chances are he figured it out for himself. He was a weak one, an' a damned fool. That kind don't live long, Buchman. He fell in with crooks, an' he was a crook himself. There's his story."

Trev nodded. All three were gone now, and the world was a better place without them.

McTigue said laconically, "Somebody comin' up from the Wyoming Belle, Buchman."

Trev moved away from him, then, walking down the street, walking faster and faster as he recognized Rhoda Greene coming toward him, hatless, hurrying.

She saw him, and she let out a small, glad cry.

"Trev," she whispered. "Trev."

He held her tightly in his arms. "All-over," he said. "All over."

It was over, but it was beginning, too. It was the beginning of something else which would be finer, better, more beautiful, and it would be forever.

William Heuman was born in Brooklyn, New York. In 1938 he went to work with the National Supply Corporation as a clerk and over the next twelve years wrote Western short stories extensively for the magazine market. What is most notable in these early stories is Heuman's subtlety in plotting. If the outcome of a particular tale was never in doubt, Heuman could generate quite a lot of tension as to just how the outcome would be reached, and he was usually able to include a surprise twist at the end. In 1950 Heuman published his first original paperback Western novel, *Guns at Broken Bow*. The secondary characters really help to carry this story, as had long been the case in Heuman's short fiction, providing a vivid background for the main conflict between a former lawman seeking peace and a place to take up cattle ranching. By the time the book appeared, Heuman was generating sufficient income from writing Western fiction to retire from his commercial job and concentrate full-time on writing. Throughout the 1950s and 1960s, Heuman continued annually to produce two, three, and some years even four original paperback Westerns while simultaneously continuing his production of short novels and stories for pulp magazines. *The Range Buster* (1954) and *Heller from Texas* (1957) are outstanding novels with traditional settings from this period, but he also could and did produce stories with more exotic elements such as keelboating in *Keelboats North* (1953), a Tennessee mountain man in New Mexico in *On to Santa Fe* (1953), fighting Sioux Indians and winter weather in *Wagon Train West* (1955), riverboating in *Ride for Texas* (1954), and stagecoach robberies in *Stagecoach West* (1957). Heuman can be described as a consistently entertaining author of Western fiction, with colorful stories and interesting characters. His heroines are often very strong characters, women who manage their own ranches and occasionally a stageline, who are never helpless in the face of adversity and who frequently provide essential assistance to the protagonist without which he would be lost. The consistent quality of his Western fiction remains extraordinary.